What the Wind Blew In

LYNNE PULIZZI

Cover design and interior formatting by:

King's Custom Covers

www.KingsCustomCovers.com

ISBN: 979-8551169543

First Edition: November 2020

10 9 8 7 6 5 4 3 2 1

Dedications

To all the people who helped me get the book done Kirsten Pomerantz for editing and Caytlin Cole for going through it and putting it into book form from basically one long run on sentence. Also thanks to everyone out there who is willing to read this story.

I hope you like it.

Chapter 1

S eth was the lucky person picked for the watch that night. Being a wind watcher was a great job most of the time, but sometimes it could get really exciting. No one ever knew what the wind would be blowing in or when it would blow.

As Seth sat there pondering what might happen, there was one story that was really making its presence known to him this night, the one that old Shuska would tell to all the children.

Old Shuska who was the eldest in the village, told of how one night, long ago, when the people had just come to this place, there were balls of lights floating around that seemed friendly and the people had become mesmerized by the lights. All the people of the tribe would come together and watch the dancing lights with their long swirls that had the colors of the rainbow with twinkling stars falling into the streamers trailing off. The people would rejoice at their twinkling, dancing and singing in their resplendent beauty.

Then one night it all changed.

It was a night when the two moons looked as if they were falling to the ground, one on top of the other. That had always been a night of great sorrow for the people. But this night proved to be the most sorrowful of all as the dancing lights came twinkling into view. One by one, the dancing people disappeared as the wind began to blow and the mist rose from the land, they were never seen again. The people who were left cried for the loss of their loved ones and to this day nobody has ever known what happened to the old ones of long ago.

As Seth sat mulling this story over and over in his mind, the lights came into view one by one. The twinkling lights became swirls. He started to get really scared and the sweat started to bead on his forehead as he heard the distant music of the lights calling him. At first softly, then louder and more compelling as he resisted. He had been warned of this; his big brother said this happened to some of the watchers.

Some didn't feel anything or see anything but there were a few like Seth and his family who could hear and feel the lights. Being a feeler had its advantages, but in a way it put him in much more danger than the other watchers. He had to be careful the lights didn't take him. A few had disappeared since that fateful night and all who disappeared had been the feelers and the hearers. The ones who weren't strong. Seth wasn't about to become one of them.

The moons were almost up now and the wind was picking up to a dull roar. Seth pulled his coat tighter around him and took out his blanket. At least he didn't have to be totally uncomfortable tonight. His mother had packed him some bread and cheese so he took it out and started to eat a chunk of cheese. It was his favorite. A nice mild kind that melted in his mouth.

His mother was a master cheese maker and his father was a shepherd. The goats they raised were known for their milk, and for their long hair. His family was well praised for the quality of the hair. Weavers from all over would trade for the hair. Seth and his family were well clothed because of that, but his mother's cheese was the best. It was her own recipe and only his sister would learn how to make it when she was old enough. Swela was only five so it would be awhile. All she wanted to do was play and pester her mother. Seth at this moment was wishing very hard that he was only five and tucked into his bed, sleeping quite happily.

But the reality was he was on his first watch and scared to death.

Now the lights were really swirling and whirling so fast he would get dizzy if he stared too long. The music called and the wind howled and howled. Then in came something on the wind as the lights rushed to meet it. Seth couldn't see exactly what it was. He was really wishing it wouldn't be another dragon though. Maybe it was just an illusion, but deep in his bones he knew it wasn't. He also knew that he would have to be responsible for whatever the wind blew in during his watch. It seemed small enough and not too threatening. Maybe he'd be lucky. At least he could hope. Then out of the lights she came walking, slow and deliberate, right towards him.

Seth was so scared he didn't know what to do. This had never happened to anyone before. Not ever that he knew of, at least. Then there she was! She seemed safe except for all the twinkling lights swirling around her. She was small and definitely not one of the people. Her eyes were big and slanted and her ears had delicate points. She had long silver hair and bluish silver skin. Her clothes were something Seth had never seen before. The cloth was so fine you could almost see through it. The shifting of the cloth was hypnotic. Seth was feeling very confused. On one side he was petrified and on the other side he wanted to worship her.

He just sat there and stared. He didn't move, he didn't even dare breathe. As she walked toward Seth she held his gaze. To her, Seth seemed big and bulky, not at all like her. His curly brown hair, smooth light brown skin and big blue eyes made him one of the good looking people. Those were inherited traits in his family; they all looked alike. Even his mother and father looked alike.

But as Seth gazed at her with all the lights swirling, all he could think was how different and wonderful she was, and so unafraid of the lights. The lights were almost touching him now, and all his fear welled up inside him at once as the lights sang and sang. Then there was silence. So complete and total not even a blade of grass moved. Seth noticed the wind had stopped, too. The swirling, twinkling lights slowed, and the greens and yellows separated into bright twinkling lights brighter and stronger than before. Then she spoke, her words floated across the air like a gentle summer's wind, murmuring down the slopes to the lakes with no bottoms. At first, Seth had no idea what she said. All he knew was that he was spellbound. Slowly the words began to penetrate. She had asked him who he was and why he was alone, watching the beautiful lights.

As they talked, Seth began to calm down enough to start making some sense of what was being said. He found out her name was Miranda and that the wind had indeed blown her in. That was good to know. At least she wasn't some illusion the lights had made to lure him away into the fields, to be lost forever.

Miranda, it seemed, had come from where the dragons lived. She looked about Seth's age and wasn't quite sure about things either, but she did know the lights were friendly enough and wouldn't hurt her. She couldn't understand why Seth was so terrified of them. All this time, Seth was thanking his lucky stars that Miranda was so nice, and that the wind had chosen someone so beautiful to blow in. As the night passed, they talked with the lights swirling and dancing around them until the dawn came.

There was no wind for the rest of the night. As the sun rose, the blue light of the sun got brighter. Noises from the tribe started drifting toward them. Miranda became quieter, and she was starting to look worried.

She asked Seth, "What will happen now? Will everybody be afraid of me because I came in on the wind? Will they be friendly?"

He could tell how frightened she truly was. All Seth could do was shrug his shoulders. Nobody had ever brought back a person that the wind had blown in. They'd found all types of strange animals and plants, but not people.

Now it was time.

Seth gathered up his belongings as the last of the lights faded, took a deep breath and said, "Let's go and see."

Miranda knew she was the first person that had been blown in by the wind, and she was a little afraid now, too. But off they trudged to the village. That's what they called it, although it was a group of about 20 families who just sort of came together a couple of generations ago on the edge of the field of lights. It seemed there would be lots of excitement today and probably no work would get done as soon as everyone saw Miranda.

They were getting pretty close to the first house now. It was the Miller's house. There were sleepy kids coming out of the house for chores, and animals making all sorts of hungry noises. Then Sen, who was one of Seth's closest friends, saw them coming down the path. Sen came racing over, almost falling over himself in the process. His eyes were as big as saucers as he just stared at Miranda who in turn met his gaze with level calmness, although that wasn't at all what she was feeling.

Seeing all these giant people was very unnerving to her, even though she could sense that they meant her no harm.

Sen said, "Is this what the wind blew in? Boy are you lucky."

By now the rest of the family had gathered and were all staring at Miranda. She was beginning to feel quite uncomfortable and was trying to hide behind Seth. All the noise was just too much for her. Seth was trying to quiet everyone down, which was only working somewhat, but eventually everybody quieted enough to hear what Seth was trying to say.

First he introduced Miranda to everybody one by one, which took some time, because there were eight children and two parents.

Jan and Myella, Sen's parents, were as much in awe of Miranda as their children. They kept calm and politely asked if Seth and Miranda would like some breakfast after being out all night. The smells from the house were inviting, but Seth said "no thank you." He thought he'd better be getting home and hoped to see everybody at the village meeting today. He knew the whole village would like to meet Miranda.

So off they went, but this time avoiding people until they reached Seth's home.

His parents, Ty and Joel, were happy to see their son back and then they noticed Miranda, who was hanging back and trying to hide behind Seth.

Joel asked Seth, "Is this what the wind blew in?" Seth just nodded. Then there was silence.

Ty finally said, "Let's go in and talk about this." So in they went.

The only one who seemed truly excited was Swela. Miranda was only about a head taller than her, and Swela thought she had a new playmate. Swela soon was very disappointed because Miranda seemed only interested in talking to the big people and wasn't paying much attention to her at all. So off she trounced like a wounded kitty to pout, and left all the big people to themselves.

Meanwhile, Ty and Joel were asking Seth what had happened. Seth told the story of how Miranda had gotten here and how the lights had swirled around her all night and the lights were swirling around him while they talked also. His parents were truly scared. They knew the prophecy of long ago, but had not told any of their children. All the grown-ups knew, but no one ever told the children until the children had children and they were safe. Now it seemed no one was safe. So Seth and Miranda sat and listened as the prophetic legend was told.

One day a boy child would be born who could hear and feel the lights. The lights would be his friends and the winds would bring him a companion from a far-off land who would share in his learning and questing for the lost people. The lights would take them to the people and bring them back to their home. That was only part or the prophecy, as the rest had not been known by any of the people.

This sent chills up and down both Seth's and Miranda's backs and Miranda began to cry. She had thought when the wind came back that it would blow her home again. She had just been looking at this as a grand adventure to tell her friends and family when she got home. Now she wasn't so sure she'd ever get home.

Seth had told her the story of the lights and how they had tricked the people into the field to dance with them and how the wind had carried them off to an unknown place. This was what the people of the village had thought happened. Miranda had just poo-pooed it. Now, she wasn't so sure. Joel came over and put her arms around Miranda and gave her a long, warm hug. Seth was pretty shaken up, but he was trying to be brave about it.

Ty said, "Why don't we all get some breakfast?"

Seth's older brother, Sal, got up and went to the cupboard to get plates and cups and Ty went to the stove to dish up the potatoes and eggs that had almost been forgotten. Joel was still holding Miranda, and when the smell of food made Miranda's stomach growl everybody started to laugh. Even Swela forgot she was pouting.

After a good breakfast of eggs and potatoes with some lush berries for dessert, things didn't seem quite so bad. Miranda told them how she had been out walking on the cliffs by her home when a great wind had come and swept her away. She had heard of those things happening, but she never thought it would happen to her. Then the lights had swirled around her and brought her safely to the ground. The wind ride was probably the most exciting thing that had ever happened to her, but she was worried her parents would think she was dead and miss her. Seth said maybe the lights could somehow tell her parents.

That was a new idea. Nobody had ever thought of trying to talk to the lights before.

Both Ty's and Joel's eyes shone with pride as they listened to their son talk of how this might work. Seth thought that, if you could hear the lights then, they could maybe hear you and, being lights, could fly faster than a bird. Since Miranda didn't know where she was in relation to her home, just maybe the lights could find her home. So it was agreed that tonight they would try this, at least.

Now the council had to be told that the prophecy was to be fulfilled. Sal was sent to tell the council in the village what was going on at there home.

Chapter 2

Seth still couldn't see why he had to go rescue people who should have been dead over four hundred years ago, but his parents said it was for the council of elders to decide what was to be done. By the time he and Miranda went outside, they could hear the commotion in the village. Nothing exciting ever happened in the village except for the occasional peddler coming through for trade, and this was no peddler!

Sen and his family had already spread the word. Everybody was already gathered in the village square, waiting. Even Seth's girlfriend, Fern, was there. She wanted to see who this mysterious blue girl was.

As Seth's family came walking up, all eyes turned to stare at Miranda. The old ones who knew the prophecy looked sad and frightened all at the same time. The children just stared at Miranda. The village was a small one with a village square. Any trading was done amongst the people themselves, and if a traveling peddler would come into the village, he would just set up in the square.

It was a clean village, with all the houses made of stone with thatched roofs. The houses were large and mostly had additions. Each house had a neat vegetable patch, which the children all weeded, and if the children were grown and gone, the grandchildren came to weed. There were drying racks in the yards, and each house had their own bath inside. One of the reasons the ancestors had settled here was the hot water that flowed up from the earth, so the rocks under foot were always nice and warm. It was a cheery, clean village. But now, there were mumblings and stirrings going on.

Ty and Joel stepped to the center of the square, followed by Seth and Miranda.

There was dead silence, then and Ty spoke. "You all by now have seen Miranda. She blew in on the wind last night. She's from the land where our dragon had come from. I dare say she's not really as noisy as that poor old fellow." A few scattered laughs came from the crowd. That broke some of the tension. But the adults still looked very serious.

Ty continued, "As all of the adults know, the beginning of the prophecy is being fulfilled. I don't know whether it's a blessing or a curse to go to my son and Miranda. That, I guess, will be up to the spirits. May theirs protect and guide them." There was a murmur from the crowd, and someone said they'll need it.

As Miranda looked out at all the round-eyed, round-eared, brown-skinned people, her heart sank. It didn't seem like the grand adventure she imagined and she was sure by now her parents were getting pretty worried about her. But what could she do but go on? At least nobody wanted to hurt her. So she put on her bravest face and let Ty tell the story of the prophecy for all to hear. With murmurs and approvals, the crowd accepted all that was spoken of the prophecy. Then at last one old man, Olif, who lived in the woods and was so old that nobody remembered how old he was, came forward and explained what was to be done next.

Seth and Miranda were to go with him to prepare to go into the lights so they could find their way back. That was the biggest thing: finding their way back.

Everyone trusted Olif. He lived in the forest and occasionally showed up with things to trade. He was known as an honest and fair man, though a bit odd. So it was settled—Seth and Miranda would go with Olif tomorrow and start their training. But tonight, they had something else to do—go talk to the lights. That's something no-one had ever done and lived to tell the story. So that was that. With everything settled, people wanted to know all about Miranda and where she came from.

They all seemed eager to hear, so Miranda told of her land and of the cliffs that bordered the sea. As she talked, the soft singing of her voice enchanted the village. Even the tiniest baby lay quietly in its mother's arms, listening to the soft chanting rhythm of her voice. She told of the seas and the ships that would sail into the bay and bring wonderful foods and clothes to trade with her people, and how her people would dive to the bottom of the sea to get corals of many bright colors and shapes to trade for the treasures the ships would bring. Some of the people, like her father, would make beautiful jewelry out of the coral, which the ship's captains would sometimes fight over. So Miranda's family was quite well off.

She herself loved to go to the cliffs and listen to the wind's song and watch the dragons flying out over the ocean. The dragons seemed to enjoy her company and would come in to get her and take her off for rides when they would notice her watching. She could talk to them, which was a rare gift among her people. When she had heard of how the wind had blown a dragon to this place and that he had howled for days, she'd almost fallen over laughing because that dragon was Milos and he was sort of a bully, so to hear he was scared was totally hilarious to her.

Seth and the village hadn't thought so. Nobody could sleep a wink with him around, and everybody was glad when the winds took him away.

The wind was capable of bringing and taking things from different dimensions and then dropping things in other dimensions. Nobody knew how that happened; they just knew it happened because it had happened to the people in the old times. The villagers never questioned it. It just was what their reality was.

Miranda told of their homes, which were made of thin sheets of a stuff she called *tolmoic*, which let the light in, so you could not see in, only see out. The houses were sturdy against the strong winds that blew off the ocean. The *tolmoic* collected the heat during the day and kept the houses warm at night. Not one house had blown down in over five hundred years.

As she described her homeland, her thoughts raced. The thing she thought she'd miss most was her bed. It was made of the softest feathers and silk you could get. Her father had traded a ship's merchant two coral necklaces and matching bracelets for it. Now she was afraid she would never see it again, or her family. She had four brothers who were going to be jewelers, too. She hadn't worried about herself yet.

She had known that one day her destiny would show itself. In the meantime, she had the dragons to play with, but to be swept away from them by the wind and to go off adventuring with a strange looking young man was definitely not anything she had imagined.

By the time she had finished her story, the village had fallen in love with her, even Fern, despite herself.

Chapter 3

The day had started out nice enough, but as Miranda finished her story, clouds were gathering overhead, and in the distance they heard the rolling claps of thunder coming through the hills surrounding the little village. Everyone decided it was best to disperse and go home to finish up the day's chores in short order before the rain came.

The young boys were glad no goats would be out today. They could stay and play their favorite game of *Twissling*, where two boys team up against two other boys. One team has a spinner and the other team has the twissle stones. The spinners have to knock the twissle out of the ring, the object was for the spinners to knock the stones out of the gaming space and for the boys who had the stones to keep them in the gaming space. It was almost like a festival day. But soon the rain would be here and, with it, the winds again.

Sen had volunteered to watch tonight. Somewhere in the back of his brain, he hoped another Miranda would blow in. He didn't think it would really happen, but he wanted to watch anyway. Seth was his best friend and he knew Seth would be out trying to talk to the lights. Sen wanted to be there in case anything might happen to Seth and Miranda.

People were heading home now. Fern caught up to Seth and Miranda and asked what was going to be happening tonight. As Miranda explained, Sen joined them and the four of them started off down the road. By the time they got to Seth's house, Miranda had completely won over Fern. It seemed these two were going to be friends despite the size difference. Fern was tall and well built, a big sturdy farm girl. Her face was pretty and she had her own look about her. She had the same blue eyes as Seth's family and light brown skin. Her hair was straight and thick and hung to her waist. Now it was blowing in the wind and she wished she had braided it today.

The path swung down the hill and around the curve was Seth's house. There was a big circle of old oak trees surrounding it. Their garden was a big one, and Joel, Seth's mother, was already securing things for the storm. It looked to be a big storm and she didn't want any of the vegetables to get ruined. The four friends pitched in to help. But this time Miranda surprised everyone by holding up her hands and creating a clear dome orb of energy over the whole garden. When everyone stopped and stared in astonishment, she turned — a shade of darker blue. She tried to explain that's what they did to protect their gardens from the winds of the sea. She told them the rain could still get through but it was slowed down so it didn't hurt the plants. The wind just blew around it. Miranda said everybody could do it where she came from.

Joel invited everyone inside for some tea and some cheese with bread because it was lunchtime. Fern declined, saying she had to get home and help her folks before the storm hit. Sen stayed; he would not pass up a chance to eat some of Joel's cheese, even if it meant putting up with Swela, Seth's little sister, who would be climbing all over him. As everyone was sitting to eat, the conversation started to turn towards what Olif would teach them. Who was he, really?

He had always kept to himself and lived out in the woods all alone. How would he even have known about Miranda arriving here? So as the conversation twisted through the questions, more of the legend was told to Seth, Sen, and Miranda. Seth's parents seemed to know a lot about Olif and were comfortable with letting him and Miranda go and learn with him.

The legend said, *Olif was one of the wise ones. He was a baby when the wind came and the people were lost and that was four hundred years ago. He was ancient beyond anyone's life spans now. It was said he would live until the prophecy was fulfilled, and then he could go to his rest. Olif is the only one who knows the key to the coming and going of the lights. When the people of long ago were taken, the lights left a key. The key could not be used by the caretaker of the people or it would be lost forever.*

"So old Olif has lived waiting for the prophecy to come true," Ty said, "and now here are the two of you."

Sen said, "Three of us." He had no intention of staying and letting his best friend go adventuring with a beautiful creature like Miranda without him.

Ty said, "That is for Olif to decide, for only he has the key. Only he knows who could enter and come home again." So, as much as Sen hated it, it would be Olif's decision.

With lunch out of the way and the storm almost on top of them, Sen thought he'd better get home and get ready for the wind watch tonight. Seth was getting plain ol' tired and wanted some sleep. Miranda was exhausted, too. Joel sent Seth off to bed and started to take Miranda off to the extra room when the storm crashed right on top of the house. As tired as she was, Miranda lay there for a few minutes listening to the storm as she drifted off to sleep.

When she awoke, the rain had turned to a light drizzle and it was almost dusk.

Miranda heard noises from other parts of the house, so she got up to investigate. Swela was hanging all over her Mom, wanting a story. Sal was starting to help with dinner. Seth was already up and had their dinner packed. It was time to go to the lights again. But this time Sen would be there too, and so would Miranda.

Miranda got ready. She had a drink of Zoosh for extra energy, and off they went, back down the path, but this time they didn't have to hide. Everyone was inside sheltering from the rain. Seth was getting soaked, but Miranda barely had a drop on her. That started to annoy Seth.

Finally, he asked her why and she said, "You know the bubble over your garden. Well, a smaller bubble is more concentrated, so less rain can get in. Would you like to try?" So in walked Seth. It was like walking through a wall of soup, but on the inside it was warm and dry. Seth was amazed.

By the time they got to the ledge, Sen was there, and he was soaked too. Seth was almost dry. Sen was wondering why or how those two could keep so dry, then Miranda wrapped him in the bubble, too. At first Sen was scared as the thick soup encircled him, but all of a sudden, he was warm and dry. His round eyes got rounder as he stared at Miranda. But in the next instant the lights appeared, and all eyes were on the lights. In the next second a breeze sprang up, at first gentle, then hard and heavy.

Without the bubble, Sen would have been even colder than Seth was last night. But in a warm dry bubble with friends, it was fun.

The twinkling lights were starting to swirl their green and yellow lights and Sen froze. He had done the watch once before, but it was very uneventful. The lights had only twinkled far off in the field, staying out there, and the wind hadn't blown anything in. But tonight, the greens and yellows swirled together, making lovely patterns and Seth could hear them calling; so could Miranda.

Sen couldn't hear a thing, which was good for him. Otherwise, he'd be gone before he knew what hit him. That's what had happened to Jessy, one of the other watchers. He took off like that when the lights were acting up. He never was quite the same after that. Well, Sen couldn't hear, so he was safe, at least for a time. But Seth and Miranda could hear.

Miranda went to the edge of the bubble and called the lights to come. At first they were surprised, people had never tried to speak to them before, so some lights came swirling up, twinkling as they came to investigate. Sensing Miranda, the lights covered her, Seth, and Sen. Sen was terrified, but Seth and Miranda just stood there. Sen didn't know what else to do, so he just stayed, too.

The lights picked and probed, then started to ask and call again.

Then Miranda asked, "Can you take a message to my parents?"

"Yes, yes," the lights whispered, but only to those who heard.

So Miranda asked, "Will you take a message to my parents?"

"Yes, yes," was all they replied.

Miranda put a picture of herself and what happened to her into her mind and the lights picked it up and made the same images within themselves. Next she asked the lights to take the message to her home which she pictured in her mind also. Then she would wait for an answer.

In the next instant, one light shot off into the night. The other lights stayed and danced. Others hovered around the three people in the bubble. By now the wind was a howling, roaring monster, tearing down the slope and the next thing they all knew, something was coming out of the field, like last night.

But it wasn't small like Miranda. It was big. Really big. With wings.

Miranda ran from the bubble straight toward the creature. Seth and Sen were too scared to move. As Miranda ran toward it, huge wings opened as if to scare her and Miranda was shouting, "Metuluso how did the wind bring you here, too?"

The big dragon looked down at the tiny Miranda and sighed. "Your parents have been worried sick over you and blaming us for your disappearance. We tried to tell them it must have been the wind, but they won't listen. Come, hop on my back and I'll take you home."

By now, Seth and Sen had managed to overcome their fear and go investigate, even if it was in the middle of the field of lights.

Miranda said, "No, I have a few things I have to do here first." And she told the dragon that a message had been sent to her parents, through the lights, telling them where she was. If Metuluso would like to stay, she would love to have her come with them.

Metuluso sighed again and said, "It would probably be best if I stayed to protect you, or your parents would have a royal fit if I were to leave without you."

All the pieces of the prophecy where coming together: the three portal hoppers, Seth, Miranda, and Sen; their protector Metuluso; and the portal keeper Olif, their teacher.

To Sen's great amazement, he was included!

Chapter 4

Metuluso was huge. Her golden eyes were as big as Seth's head. She had long pointed teeth that stuck out the edges of her mouth, and two very large pointed horns growing out the top of her head. Her skin was a smooth blueish green, which was really quite pretty. Miranda was standing in the middle of the field, hugging Metuluso's ankle, which was about as tall as Miranda. Seth and Sen almost reached the bottom of the dragon's knee. Both Seth and Sen were totally in shock. Their minds were numb.

Never had either of them seen any living creature so massive. The other dragon the wind blew in was a bit smaller, and much louder. Metuluso was very dignified and was resigned to take care of Miranda through this foolishness.

By now the lights were in a total frenzy. Blinking, whirring, and calling, "Come, come, come…" but nobody noticed them.

Metuluso tried to swoosh the lights away as they buzzed about her head. Then it seemed, all at once, everybody knew where they were.

Miranda said, "Maybe we should go back." They all agreed. So back they started to walk, with Metuluso taking up the rear.

The wind had died down just as it had last night, but the drizzle kept up. Miranda made another bubble and they managed to keep dry. Metuluso didn't care about the rain. As things calmed down, they began to talk again, at first slowly, then all at once.

Miranda was excited that Metuluso was there. Sen was thrilled the wind blew in this huge dragon while he was on watch. That meant he, Sen, had to watch her, for it was the responsibility of the watcher to take care of whatever had been blown in on their watch.

Metuluso looked around and rumbled. Everyone stopped talking and Metuluso started to speak. Miranda of course knew what she was saying and so did Seth, he was shocked that he could understand Dragon. Sen had no idea what Metuluso was saying, so Miranda interpreted for him.

First Metuluso wanted to know their names. After introductions went around, she asked Miranda if she would go home when the prophecy was fulfilled .

They needed her help to fulfill the prophecy, and as to what was going to happen they didn't know. Only Olif knew, or so they thought. They would find out tomorrow what they would have to do. Then they talked about what would happen when the village caught news that another dragon had blown in. This would be funny. The boys wanted her to set up a howl through the village again, like the last dragon. But Metuluso wouldn't lower herself to howling. Finally she did agree to fly them all to town.

As dawn came and the lights faded, they all climbed on her back and took off. What an experience to lift off the ground! Miranda was in front and the two boys hung on with all their might to the bone ridges going down her back.

As Metuluso rose in the air they could see for miles and miles. The meadow of lights seemed tiny as the big forest surrounded it.

Miranda felt right at home on Metuluso's back. She had spent most of her life with the dragons. Seth and Sen were so amazed at flying that all they could do was hang on and look as the wind blew through their hair and the earth became a tiny speck below.

Before they knew it, the ride was over and they were at Seth's house. With the landing of Metuluso, the farm animals became hysterical—they felt sure they would become the dragon's dinner. The noise drew Ty and Joel out to see what was going on.

By now, not much startled them, but having a twenty-foot dragon waiting in their front yard was a bit much even for them. As they looked at Metuluso's big golden eye's swirling with the lights of thousands of years, they knew.

In their hearts, Seth, Miranda, and Sen knew they would be safe and guided by the spirits. By now, the whole family was outside and Swela was so excited to see the dragon. She ran right up to her and started to pet her foot, since that was all she could reach.

Metuluso looked down at her and gave her a little nudge with her nose so she would look at her. When Swela saw the swirling lights in those big golden eyes, she squealed in delight and hugged the enormous head of the dragon.

Never had Metuluso met a human with so much love in her heart and with no fear. She was amazed at this pure love that came out of such a small child that she gave her the blessing of the dragons. This was a rare gift to bestow on anyone. With this gift, Swela got the gift to speak to and learn from the dragons. She became the first human to ever get that honor.

"Swela is too young to learn the knowledge of the dragons — but when she is old enough I shall return to teach her our ancient knowledge," Metuluso, through Miranda, told Seth's parents.

By now, the whole village was gathering at their house to see what the ruckus was about. This time, Sen's parents were looking pretty worried. They knew Sen was now responsible for this huge dragon that the winds had blown in. Deep in their hearts, they knew that they, too, would be losing their son to the prophecy.

Chapter 5

Seth's parents were sitting in their house with very mixed feelings. They were very proud of their children, yet they were very upset that their children's destiny would lead them away from the village.

The next day it was time to go. Olif had left the day before for reasons unknown to the village.

Joel had packed lots of bread and cheese and vegetables for Seth to take to Olif's house. She wanted to make sure everybody would get enough to eat.

That was her job.

Olif had said that the children would be at his house for at least four weeks if everything went well.

He lived deep in the forest and it would be a long hike to his house. Everyone was expecting at least two days to get there, but they had forgotten that Metuluso could fly them there in a matter of a few hours. Joel was starting to get teary as the children were gathering up their clothes and they had rounded up some clothes for Miranda from the neighbors so she wouldn't have to wear the same things for a month.

They had slept well into the afternoon, after being up all night. By the time they woke, it was already warm and sunny.

The weather was about the same everyday, with the exception of the occasional storm that blew through and the wind in the meadow that blew things in, which wasn't part of the normal weather. The winds that blew things in was something else that nobody could explain. The two moons stabilized the planet, and the blue-white star gave them a wonderful, warm heat. They were quite comfortable where they lived.

The warm water that flowed under the village gave everybody hot water to bathe in. The villagers were very clean people compared to the people from the north, who hardly bathed at all.

Nobody knew what Olif's house looked like. Only one or two people had been there and that was a long time ago. Their stories about his place kept changing over time; nobody knew for sure what it really was like.

He had lived there for four hundred years and had never left except to come to the village market to trade or sell the things he made for things he needed. He always knew when the traders were coming to the village, just as he seemed to know about Miranda showing up in the wind.

Nobody knew how he would always know these things. He just did, it was like he heard it on the wind.

The children were a little worried about what they would find there, none of them had ever been away from their homes for a long period of time. Seth and Sen were ready for an adventure because they had never had one bigger than going to the next village with their parents for the annual harvest festival.

The thought of flying on Metuluso again made them giddy with excitement. Miranda, on the other hand, was excited but was starting to miss her home and family and friends, but she knew that the lights had taken the message to her parents and she was sure that someone would hear the lights.

The time had come when everything was ready and everybody climbed up on Metuluso's back. Metuluso lowered her front knee to the ground so the group could climb up. Then she waited till the boy's had a good grip on her. With a powerful lunge and wing beat she was up and off the ground in a swirl of blue and green.

It was quite a sight to see and even more exciting to be on her back. Miranda was used to flying with Metuluso. She was so happy that at least someone from her home was with her. As they climbed higher in the sky, they could see the village disappear below them, then there were only green trees. There was a thick rich green cover on the ground as the forest below thickened.

For about an hour, all they saw was forest, and they were really glad that they were flying and not walking. Seth and Sen were starting to get sore legs and bottoms from sitting and rubbing against the dragon's skin. The beautiful blue-green skin had tiny scales that started to rub into their legs and the bony spine was not very comfortable either. Miranda wasn't bothered in the least. She had her bubble of energy that cushioned her just enough to be quite comfortable and happy.

There was no talking as the wind rushed by. The sound just drowned out to nothing.

After about another hour, the forest started to thin. Over to the left they saw a peaceful cottage by a stream with a little waterfall coming around a bend. The grass was almost the same dark green as the trees, and there was a huge garden and a barn to keep the animals in.

There also was a dog running around who had seen the dragon and was going nuts with excitement. There was no fear in her, or any of the other animals, like there had been when Metuluso had landed at Seth's house.

As she saw the cottage, Metulusoe started to circle down to the ground. By the time she landed, she was grinning from ear to ear, with her lips curled up and dancing and her tail wagging so hard that her whole body was wagging. Seth and Sen had never seen a dog that happy.

Miranda jumped off the dragon and ran over to her saying, "Kali, how did you get here?"

Seth and Sen just looked at her, wondering how she knew Kali. Miranda was very bewildered by it, too. Olif came out of the cottage at that moment. He didn't even look surprised that they had gotten there so fast.

Instead, he just said, "I'm so glad that you all could make it so quickly. We have lots of work to do."

Then Miranda blurted out, "How did Kali get here?!" She was truly surprised that her dog, her best friend, was here at her side.

Olif was old and not one to mince words. He told her she came through the portal. Miranda wanted to know what portal and why, so Olif had to explain about the portal before anything else happened.

The portal connects one dimension to the next dimension. When the lights had gone to find Miranda's parents to tell them where she was, her parents insisted on sending Kali to be with her to protect her.

Kali was almost as big as Miranda. She had brindle fur and a white stripe up the middle of her forehead that ended in a star on the top, with a tail that never stopped wagging.

Olif was a very kind, old man. All the animals loved him, and Kali was no exception. Metuluso was also impressed with him.

Olif told them, "After four hundred years, you come to see that the world, and all other dimensions, are about love. Nothing more and nothing less."

By then Seth was starting to see something that wasn't making sense to him.

Miranda was from another dimension. Which meant that Metuluso and Kali were also from another dimension. Seth just started to say what he had figured out when Sen jumped in and said it.

Miranda explained how her dimension was different then theirs. Her dimension was the Realm of Fairies, Elves and Dragons. Seth and Sen's dimension was the Realm of Humans and Mammals. Their dimension was without magic. The elves and fairies had magic.

Sometimes, these dimensions would come together and that's when the winds blew things from dimension to dimension. Like the field at the village where Seth and Sen live. At a certain point where the energies come together and are connected it is at that point where a portal will appear and that is right here where they are right now. From what anyone can tell that point is the same in all dimensions.

Seth and Sen were beginning to get the picture, but it was a little much for them. Fortunately, they were brave young men and had open minds about most things. When it came to solid evidence, there were Metuluso, Miranda, and Kali. You couldn't dispute that. Or the dragon rides.

So there it was: different dimensions.

The next logical question was how many dimensions there were. Olif said he had access to thirteen through his portal. Miranda said she didn't know how many because she just knew the winds blew you around and you never knew where you would end up. Only the lights knew where the portals were.

Olif was the only one in their dimension who had the knowledge of controlling which dimension you ended up at. He was the only keeper of the portal in this dimension; the lights had been able to tell

Miranda's parents which dimension she was in and they happened to know the portal keeper in her home and sent Kali through to Olif.

Kali wasn't just the happy-go-lucky dog that she appeared to be. Coming from the land of fairies and elves she too had magical powers, and that is why she was sent to Miranda. Nobody knew where the lost people were or what they would encounter on their quest for them. Kali had been assigned as ground protection in case anything would try to harm the children. It was her parent's idea and Olif agreed that she would be a great asset to their group. She could sense danger from far off and could see in all realms.

She could also dart in and out of these realms as fast as a blink of an eye. She was not afraid to attack to protect those she loved if they were in danger.

Chapter 6

O lif told the four travelers he would show them to their rooms so they could put their bags down. Then, as soon as they were settled in, he would show them around. So off everybody went into the cottage with Olif in the lead. Metuluso of course couldn't follow, so she settled down in the yard for a quick nap.

As they entered the cottage, they were surprised at how big it was. There was an entryway that had big, thick beams and two benches, all made out of the same light brown wood that looked like honey. The floors were a polished lava rock that almost looked like a mirror, and reflected the light that filtered in through the windows. They were made out of a clear hard substance that Seth and Sen had never seen before.

They wanted to know what it was and Miranda told them it was a special rock called *tolmoic* that came from her home. All their houses were made from it. Olif had gotten it through the portal at different times in his life.

As for Olif, he was over four hundred years old but looked like he was about fifty. He looked old enough to gain respect when he spoke, and yet he was in good enough shape to do all the work around the cottage and keep things going. He was a strong, well-built man with leathery skin which was a deep rich brown. He, too, had curly brown hair like Seth, and sky blue eyes. He could have been Seth's father, they looked so much alike.

Everyone followed Olif into the main room, a large room, which had rooms going off on eight sides. Some of the rooms had doors; others were left open and gave the place an airy feel. The ceiling had the same light brown timbers that the entryway had.

The timbers rose to a point in the center of the ceiling with a huge egg-shaped dome of light that was a sky blue with flecks of white, orange, and pink twinkling in it.

Everyone wanted to know what the dome was made of.

Olif told them that it was half of a dragon eggshell that came from one of the other dimensions, not where Miranda came from. The eggs, after they hatched, were this color and would absorb the sunlight. At night it gives off enough light to light the entire room. The outside of the eggshell looked like an opal shining in the middle of the night.

Olif promised that the group would have plenty of opportunities to look at it. He used it as a beacon to come home to if he was out after dark. He also explained that the dragons from that dimension grew on and fed off of the light. They didn't need anything else to survive.

This totally amazed all the group. Kali, of course, didn't pay any attention. Instead, she was busy running around, smelling everything, poking her nose into whatever she could. Miranda noticed her and called her over. She listened, even though a little reluctantly.

As they all gazed around the room, each one of them began to notice things that they knew as well as things that none of them had ever seen before. Miranda saw a crystal in the corner of the great room that was as tall as her. It sang with the vibration of the earth and helped to connect the dimensions. There was a warm white glow about it that sang to the heart. Miranda caught her breath at the sight of it.

There was only one place that those crystals were found, and that was in the dragonlands of her home. They were very rare and very hard to get. The only way you got one was if the dragons let you pass and if the crystal called to you. The crystal had to pick you. If you were lucky enough to obtain one, you became partnered to the crystal, which meant you could travel to any dimension you wanted to and find your way home again by the heart song of your crystal. Olif told everyone that was the crystal that was left in the field when everyone was blown away that fateful night.

Miranda asked Olif if he knew where the crystal had come from. He told her no, when the people were blown away he was just a baby. Also now he himself wasn't allowed to travel through the dimensions because he was the keeper of the portal and none of the keepers are allowed to leave. If something evil were to try to come through, he had to be there to stop it. Also, if something came through the portal by accident and was lost, he had to be there to save it.

The portals were different from the winds and lights. A portal could be used to send things and messages or people to a specific destination. By contrast, the winds just blew randomly, and took things wherever they happened to go. If you were unlucky enough to be caught by them, you never knew what would happen next.

The only way Metuluso had found Miranda was through her heart song, which is the vibration of the soul being.

Every living being has a heart song and those heart songs can link with another heart song of another being through love. That's how the two had been linked at birth and dragons can harness the winds to ride them and can talk to the lights. Where Miranda came from, all the elf children were linked with dragons.

It was pretty interesting to see the pairing take place. As the baby elves and their dragon are born within minutes of each other, they are immediately placed in the energy bubble of the parents making. A bond is formed between the two of them and, as dragon and elf grow, so does the link.

Elves and dragons can live forever, and if one gets hurt, the other can heal them. That is what the link can do, even if they are not together. So when Miranda got caught by the wind, it was fairly simple for Metuluso to find her. Miranda was one of a few elves who could talk to any of the dragon's. Usually an elf can only talk to the dragon they were bonded to.

Olif told the children that the crystal had been left when the people were taken by the winds. After they had wandered off and the light had faded, there was the crystal with the heart song of all the people in it.

It was found in the middle of the field. As the people who were left started to creep out of their hiding places, they found the crystal. It was brought to the cottage where Olif lived for safe-keeping, and eventually the village forgot about it. Olif had held it safe for four hundred years because he was the only person who remembered these people.

Kali had wandered over to investigate this crystal. She could hear the heart songs of the people. Try as she might, Miranda couldn't get her away from the crystal. Olif explained that as long as there was a heart song in the crystal, he knew the people still lived.

It was starting to get late, so Olif showed them their rooms where they would be staying while they were there. Miranda and Kali's room was small and just the right size for Miranda with furniture from where she lived, so that was just the right size for her, too. Her bed was big and low to the ground, like a big pillow on a low stand, with wooden balls holding it up off the ground. The bed was big enough for Kali to sleep on it, too. Kali loved to sleep alongside Miranda. She would cuddle up to Miranda in a little ball and sleep next to her without moving all night long.

The room was a light green, the color of new leaves in spring time. There were big windows to let in the sunlight and starlight. There was a big dresser for clothing and a bathroom with a tub to bathe in. Olif even had toilets in his house, so nobody had to go traipsing through the night to an outhouse.

Miranda was used to these things, but the boys were not. To them, they were marvelous wonders. They were used to tubs in the house, but not toilets. Olif explained how his pipes from the ground fed warm water in from the springs, and another set of pipes let the waste water out in a field away from the house, which watered that field. The boys were interested in how it all worked. Miranda really didn't care a lot, but she listened politely.

The room where the boys were to stay was next to Miranda's room, with the same big windows, and it was the color of the sky. The beds were higher off the ground and had big pillows, too. The boys were happy that they got to stay together. There was a closet for their clothes and they had their own bathroom, too.

Everyone left the clothing they brought in their rooms and Seth brought out the food that his Mom gave him and gave it to Olif. He was quite pleased with the cheese and bread. He knew how good the cheese was.

Olif told the children a story of how Seth's great, great, great, great grandmother had discovered how to make this cheese. It was quite by accident when one day she had forgotten to take the soft cheese out of its cloth and then remembered several days later when she opened the ball of cheese and tried it there was a sharp tangy flavor to the cheese. Seth and Sen had forgotten that Olif had known all those people and all the generations since.

Then Sen asked Miranda how old she was. She looked at him with a big smile and said, "Sixty of your years," and the boys' mouths dropped.

Miranda explained how time is the same in each dimension, but life in each dimension has evolved differently, so some don't age and some age very quickly. She continued to explain to them how Elves never grew old and died. They grew up really slow compared to humans. By the time she was fully grown she would be about one hundred and fifty in human years.

She also explained that elves' families are very close and tightly knit together because elves very rarely have babies. They only have a baby every three to four hundred years, so there are never many children around.

In elf years, Miranda was about their age. It still made them feel funny, though, and Olif was just laughing and laughing at them. Miranda thought it was very funny, too.

By now, everyone was getting hungry and it was time to eat. Olif had made a big pot of barley stew with tomatoes, onions, and mushrooms. For a finishing touch, he added some of the cheese to the broth and it all melted together. It smelled wonderful to all the people there, and even Kali started to beg. There were bowls stacked up by the pot and a lovely ladle made out of a deep red wood and polished to a shine that you could see yourself in. Those too had come from another dimension. All these wonders around Olif's place were great. The bread was a rich wholesome bread made from Amaranth and had a nutty taste that went great with Joel's cheese.

Everyone sat at the table to eat and nobody talked until their bowls were emptied. Seth and Sen had three helpings and Miranda had two. Olif only had one, and Kali got the leftovers.

Now the sun was starting to set and the inside of the house started to glow from the eggshell on the roof. Olif took them out to see the shell glowing. It looked like a light blue opal with swirls of pink, orange, and green light sparkling out of it. It was truly beautiful.

Miranda went over to Metuluso and asked her if she had ever heard of the dragons of light. The dimension that they came from was far above the dimension that Miranda came from. Metuluso said she had heard of them but had never met any of them. There was a legend of these light dragons that was even more ancient than Metuluso's kind. All these dimensions became too overwhelming for the boys, and even Miranda was feeling a bit confused about everything.

It was getting late and everyone was getting very sleepy. So Olif told everyone to go to bed and tomorrow they would start to learn what was needed to find the lost people. As they walked into the house, the warm glow of the eggshell lit up the house with a wonderful blue light. The boys marveled at it and Miranda just sighed in admiration.

Kali was already curled up on the bed. Miranda was not far behind. The boys went straight to their room and went to bed without so much as a peep out of them. Olif cleared up the dishes and put everything away before he went off to his room.

Chapter 7

The next day came too soon for the sleepy visitors. Kali was up exploring the room when Miranda finally woke up to the blue light of the sun streaming in through the window. It was beautiful; there were tiny rainbows bouncing around the room. As she looked, she saw tiny crystals hanging from the top of the window, which she had not seen yesterday. She yawned and stretched and Kali bounded over in one leap of joy to greet her, which made Miranda laugh at her.

As she lay in bed a few minutes and started to wake up, she started to look around the room and really study it. There were things that she had never seen before even though her father, a jeweler, traded for all sorts of things. One thing that caught her eye was a pretty lamp, which had a woman standing and holding a globe that seemed to absorb the light rather than put out light.

She decided it was time to get up. A nice bath sounded good to her. She went into the bath and started the water into the tub. Kali of course had to see what was going on. As Miranda climbed into the tub, she could hear the boys talking.

The boys had woken up with a start. Both of them had slept

like rocks and they both had forgotten where they were. After they woke up, they remembered and laughed with each other. Then they thought they would try the baths.

Sen went first, while Seth just laid in bed thinking how great it was not to have chores to do. Sen enjoyed his soak and got clean. After about twenty minutes, Sen was finished and it was Seth's turn. While Seth was soaking, Sen decided to go check on Metuluso. They had said good night, but Sen didn't know where she went to sleep.

Olif was already up making breakfast for everyone, so Sen asked him where the dragon was. He was told that she was out by the barn. There was a special place for the dragon to stay, and Olif had shown her the place. When Sen set out to check on her, he found a very large boulder next to the barn. The boulder had been hollowed out so it looked like a big cave, looking quite cozy by dragon standards. He found his charge curled up, sleeping quite soundly in that boulder. He didn't want to wake her, since he didn't know how grumpy a sleepy dragon would be.

About that time, Kali came running up to say "HI!"

She was quite happy, all smiling and tail wagging. After saying hi to Sen, she ran up to Metuluso and licked her right on the nose. This made her open one big eye, which slowly swirled browns and golds. She blinked once and went back to sleep.

Miranda came wandering up, looking breathtakingly beautiful after a good night's sleep. She had some clean clothes that her parents had sent with Kali, and she looked and felt great. She had on a pair of light green pants and matching shirt that had flowers embroidered on the sleeves with vines running up the arms. This outfit was made out of the same soft material as her other outfit. Her skin had a warm soft blue glow to it and her hair hung in soft wet waves down her back. She looked like an exotic statue that came from afar, only she was alive and breathing and happy and content.

Miranda told Sen that they had a few minutes to look around while Seth finished his bath.

As they were walking around, they looked in the barn that was next to the dragon house. It was a large stone building with a thatched roof; the inside was clean and tidy with stalls for horses and cows and a place for the chickens. There was also a pen for the goats and sheep. In the loft was all the food any animal could ever need.

Kali was off exploring and chasing things. She was just being annoying to the animals in the barn, not being threatening to them. She just wanted to play, and the older animals just tolerated her. One colt tried to butt heads with her, which made her very happy. They played together for a bit until Kali got distracted and ran off.

As they wandered through the barn, they saw a huge garden on the other side, with just about every vegetable imaginable planted in neat rows inside the beds. Pathways ran between them and there was not one weed in sight. Sen couldn't believe that. He had spent many an hour weeding his family's garden. This garden was quite a surprise.

Miranda, on the other hand, wasn't surprised at all. In her home, they had bubbles to keep the weeds out and that was what Olif had too.

Seth was done with his bath and ready for breakfast, too. Olif called everyone in to eat. There were eggs and potatoes, fresh bread and honey, fruit, and a wonderful tasting tea made from a few flowers from the herb garden.

They were all talking about the wonders of Olif's place when he interrupted them and told them that now was the time to tell them what this place was and all about himself. Everyone was very interested in what was going to be said. It became so quiet you could hear a pin drop as Olif began his story.

Chapter 8

*O*lif is the keeper of this place. It is a magical place where a portal to many other dimensions exists. The reason this place needs a keeper is to guard against anything evil coming through the opening. Also to greet the occasional guest.

In order for the keeper to do this, he needs to stay close to the portal so he can send them back quickly before anything bad can transpire.

The lights are also here to help guard against evil. But they themselves are very alien to this dimension. Their job is to distract and confuse, which they do very well, even distracting and confusing good things.

But mostly they are there to keep the balance of things. Yes, the lights are intelligent and, yes, they will carry you off if you aren't careful, but the lights themselves are good.

The cottage has been here for many, many centuries. New keepers are born every four hundred to five hundred years to take over for the last, so the previous keeper can ascend to the next level of existence. When he has passed the knowledge on to the next successor, he is free to ascend. This person or persons are born to this destiny. They have no choice—it is preordained. The keepers have been here even before the *people arrived and nobody knew where they came from. As the people arrived the original keepers transitioned the job over to the chosen ones. nobody knew when this happened. The other portal keepers that Olif knew all had the same story.*

There was a silence as what he was saying started to sink into their brains.

Sen, being the impulsive one, blurted out, "Are we the ones?"

Olif said, "It looks that way, but first you have to find the people, then we will see what fate has in store for you. That's why fate has brought the five of you together: Miranda is the user of magic; Sen is the protector; Seth is the seer and hearer; Metuluso can fly between time; and Kali senses when evil is about and will warn and protect against it.

Olif paused, then continued, "As you can see, you all are very important to this quest. It is my duty to teach each of you how to use your talents and how to work as a team to keep everyone alive to finish this very important quest."

Miranda was a little upset. She was starting to think she would *never* get home. But Olif assured her that was not the case, that if the quest is completed, there was something very special planned for her in her home.

This made her feel better. As a watcher of the portal, Olif explained that he had acquired certain magical powers, along with the whole area around the portal having magical powers.

As Olif explained about how the portal worked, he took them to the portal. It was out in a field, within sight of the house. The field looked like any other field, but it made them feel like they wouldn't want to go into it. Even Kali shied away from it, and she had come through it just yesterday. That feeling was there to protect anything from accidentally coming into the field and then getting sucked through the portal.

Olif said that the portal was always open and that things just popped through sometimes, but if you knew how to use the portal, you could pick your destination.

He said that he could never be gone for too long in case something popped through.

The children couldn't see anything, even though they were staring at the space he was pointing at. Then all of a sudden, he made a small gesture with his left hand — the air shimmered and there was the portal. It was a round, golden light with what looked like hands all around the edge, pointing into the light.

The children all gasped at once. Not even Miranda had seen anything like that. Olif explained that the portals are hidden by shifting the light and air around them to create an illusion so people don't find them. Then a repulsion spell is put in the area to keep curious people out. He said that it works quite well.

Even knowing it was there, the children didn't want to be there, and Kali just whined at the edge of the field and wouldn't go into it.

If you looked around the field, you could see every part of the farm. It was designed that way to keep an eye on things.

As everyone started to walk out of the field. All of a sudden, the golden light got brighter and the hands reached in and then out. In the hands was a bird with fiery, light feathers that looked like thousands of rainbows. Olif stopped, went back, and picked up the bewildered bird. He brought it over and showed them the bird.

He said that this bird comes from the land of the light dragons. He explained that it couldn't stay in this world for long because it needed the special light of it's dimension to live on. It was like the dragons and lived off the light energy. So now they were to get a lesson in sending something directly to a dimension and not to just wherever it happened to land.

Each dimension has a special color and symbol. You have to clear your mind to emptiness and direct the energy of the earth up through your body and out your hands to the portal, while making the symbol and saying the name.

This sounded very confusing and difficult to the two boys, but Miranda knew some of it from the magic of the bubbles. All magic stems from emptiness and earth energy; that didn't seem to vary from dimension to dimension.

So Olif showed them how to open the portal. He made it look so easy. In just a few seconds, it was open and the land shimmered, looking like it moved out of the way.

Another landscape appeared just then and the bird flew through to its home. As it took off, three feathers fell from him. All three were exactly the same size, with the light of his world caught in the feathers. They had an otherworldly opal glow to them as they floated to the ground. Olif went over to pick them up.

He walked back with a solemn but pleased look on his face and said, "You have been given a great honor. To each of you, a feather has been given by the messenger of the dragons of light. These feathers will guide you in the darkness of night or the darkness of your thoughts. You only need to look at the feather and listen for the answer you seek, and it will come to you. I will now need to have you practicing a lot of things." With that, he gave each of them a feather.

As they took their feathers, the woods took on a whole new light. The trees looked like they had different energy fields around them, with a spider's web of light connecting them to each other. Sen and Seth were truly amazed, as was Miranda, for she had heard of such things, but had never seen them. Olif explained that it was the energy that they were seeing coming from the earth, and it was that same energy that they would use to make the magic work.

Now, since they all had received this wonderful gift, their job for today was for each one to make a way to carry the feather safely and to access it easily. Olif said that the feathers will keep the light for a few days, but they need to be in the sun again to reabsorb the light or they will die. So, they needed to make a pouch that would both protect them and expose them to light.

The feathers of light could absorb light from any dimension and transmute it into the energy that sustains the life force in the feathers. The feathers also needed to stay safe. When other people saw them, they became envious and wanted them, even though they didn't know what they were.

The three of them went with Olif back to the cottage where they went into a craft room that was filled with all sorts of wonderful supplies.

All of them could make things in here, and the need to make something to protect the feathers presented itself as a great project and an opportunity for everyone to get to know each other better. Seth and Sen already were great friends, but Miranda needed to get to know them better, and nobody really knew Olif at all.

Chapter 9

A s they went in, Olif went to another room and came out with a pouch that he had made almost four hundred years ago. This pouch had a feather in it that was also from a bird of light that he had gotten his first day learning to be a keeper of the portal.

Olif's pouch had a cut-out portion that allowed light to get to the feather. It could also be turned around so other people couldn't see it. There was another pouch to keep other little things in, and there was a cord to go around the neck so it wouldn't be lost. Olif's pouch was made of a soft blue material that felt very flimsy, but was really not flimsy at all. He had sewn a design into it of a light bird sitting on a tree branch.

He told the little group that they need to sit with their feathers and close their eyes and empty their minds of all thought, and the image that came to their minds was what they needed to make.

Seth and Sen were not very good at emptying their minds; they kept thinking of everything under the sun and two moons.

Seth started to think about Fern and wondering what she was thinking about his leaving the way he did. They had barely had time to say goodbye. And what of Swela being blessed by Metuluso? What will become of her? And his parents: what would they be thinking? His mind raced in a thousand directions at once.

Then it was like someone flipped a switch and there was stillness and emptiness and darkness. Out of the darkness, came a light. At first it was small. Then it grew and took up the whole space. Out of the light, came a dragon with wings of rainbow pearl light and a body of golden light that seemed solid. His face (he somehow knew the dragon was a he) glowed with a light so intense that it almost blinded him, and he began to speak.

His voice became a hypnotic spell as he told Seth that he would be his protector on this and all journeys he would take. If he was ever in need, call his true name and he would be there, for he was a being of light and could travel instantly anywhere. Seth just needed the feather for the dragon to find him and he would be there to help Seth. As he said his true name, he was gone and there was emptiness.

Seth couldn't move; he couldn't even bring himself to open his eyes. Then his mind clicked back on and all those thousands of thoughts floated back all at once and his eyes popped open. He was back.

Miranda slipped easily into emptiness. She had learned at a young age how to do that to control the magic.

As the emptiness came, the light appeared, then split into a thousand rainbows, which were all dazzling. The colors vibrated with sound—Miranda was amazed, for she had never heard of light having sound.

She had never heard anything so beautiful in all her life. It sounded like thousands of crystals tinkling in the wind, but in a soft rhythm, not just random notes.

Then the light began to whisper, first softly then more urgently, talking all at once as one voice, as if they were surprised at someone seeing them and hearing them. These weren't the lights that had brought her here; they were from somewhere else, and she couldn't understand what they were saying, but it seemed important.

Suddenly there was silence and the world was dark, and out of the darkness came a single light that rotated from one color to the next. Then a being of light appeared. He was tall with long, silver hair that shimmered in the darkness, with long arms and legs.

He wore a robe made of light that looked like the wind was rippling it. His face was ageless. He looked like one of her people, only tall. He didn't walk—instead, he floated. When he saw that she was aware of him, he turned and started up the path that appeared, and beckoned to her to follow.

She felt no fear at all as she started up the path that wound through the darkness.

They emerged into a field of trees with people all around, and a huge yellow sun hung in the sky. The people were happy and the air was warm. It seemed like life was good for them.

Then she was back in her mind again.

Faster than you could blink, and it was over. She opened her eyes and saw a feather, her feather, lying in her hand, sparkling with all the rainbows, and a great feeling of peace came over her.

Sen, on the other hand, was having a great deal of trouble. He had never done anything like this in his life, nor had he ever tried to quiet his mind.

There was always endless chatter going through it. Usually nothing important. It seemed the harder he tried, the more his mind chattered away. He was thinking about the grand adventure and how he got to go on it and how he was on watch when the dragon blew in and what a grand dragon it was and how they got to fly on her back. He bet nobody in their village had ever gotten to fly on a dragon before.

On and on his busy mind went, when all of a sudden Metuluso's head appeared in his brain and her voice boomed, "Enough! Clear your mind." That was enough to stop thought. Then there was silence and stillness.

Metuluso took Sen's mind and linked it with hers. He was so shocked that no shield popped up and she didn't feel like a threat to him. Instead, she felt very protective and safe. After the initial shock, she gently took his mind into hers and he could see and hear through her eyes and ears.

Her memories were his memories, from her first bonding and her first flight, up to the present. As he let go and relaxed more and more, knowledge flooded his brain. He even could speak ancient Dragon, and communicate with other beings with telepathy.

Then Metuluso's mind left him and he was on his own in search of his vision. As his mind cleared, he became very still in thought. Through that stillness came a bird, like the bird that flew through the portal, only this one had long plumage that shimmered in the light. There was light all around the bird, a beautiful emerald green light, with a hint of purple floating through it.

The bird talked of his land, where time flowed at a different pace than in Sen's time. There were no nights or days—time just flowed like a river. In their dimension, things that were needed just appeared through their thoughts. Sen saw flowers so delicate that he thought that if he looked at them they would die, but the bird explained that things in this dimension neither are born nor die. They just exist.

As Sen watched, a shadow started to creep over things. The bird explained that this would be one of the challenges of finding the people: to overcome the darkness that threatened to overcome the light.

Then Sen's eyes flew open and he was Sen again, only changed a lot. He was confused about the darkness that had to be conquered for the light to come. He had always taken it for granted that the light came from the sun so this was very confusing to him.

Everyone was silent for a minute and then they all started talking at once.

Olif was smiling and said, "OK, calm down."

Sen was the most excited and he couldn't calm down, so he kept chattering on and on about being in Metuluso's mind. As he was chattering, he realized nobody knew what he was saying. He was speaking the ancient language of the dragons, and only Miranda could understand some of it.

Seth asked, "What happened to you?"

Sen just looked dumbfounded and began to speak very slowly again in Dragon.

Miranda told him that he was speaking Dragon and he needed to clear his mind and go back to his language. It took a few minutes, but he eventually got to the point where he could speak his own language again.

As Sen's story unfolded, Olif got very quiet and asked many questions about the dragons.

Dragons had a genetic memory as well as their own memory. Metuluso's memory was only of her direct lineage. But it went back to the first dragon in her dimension, and went through the whole lineage up to her. Each generation was changed a little depending on the parents.

Miranda was a little jealous of Sen because Metuluso was her bonded partner and she didn't even know that much, but she listened and learned as much about Metuluso as she could.

She found out that bonded partners couldn't be that close to each other because they wouldn't be able to be themselves, the link would be too strong. Also Metuluso linked to Sen because his mind was restless and someone had to take control of him or they all would still be waiting for him.

When he told them that, he looked a little sheepish. Just a little, though.

After about an hour of talk, Olif told them it was time to make their feather protector. They had the pick of his craft room to put whatever they wanted in or on the pouches.

There were all sorts of interesting things in the craft room to look at. Being a keeper of a portal, things got sent to him from other dimensions. He in turn, would send things out to the other places. Since keepers couldn't leave their post for very long, they traded.

Miranda found a pendant that her grandfather had made. She remembered it from when she was a very young elf, so she took it to include as part of her pouch.

There were so many different and pretty things. They were all neatly organized and put together by categories. They found cloth, but there was no leather. Nobody thought much of that, because there was so much other stuff to use. Miranda found a cloth made with many rainbows of light that reflected off the fabric. As she took it out, it shimmered and changed colors. She felt it and it was soft but strong and somehow held its shape.

Sen found some deep blue velvet material that was so soft to touch that you just wanted to keep petting it. Seth kept looking, but nothing was catching his interest or seemed right.

Then, out of the corner of his eye, he saw a soft glow that seemed inviting. As he looked closer, he saw a piece of fabric that changed colors like a chameleon. There wasn't much of it, but enough to make the pouch. There were needles and thread next to the cloth and scissors to cut with.

As they all were getting involved, Olif slipped off to get lunch started. They had all had a very busy morning. Olif went out to the garden and started getting vegetables for a salad. He picked tomatoes and lettuce and radishes and cucumbers for starters. Then he went and got some squash and eggplant.

He went into the kitchen and started making salad and vegetable kabobs that were going to be grilled over an open fire where he was roasting a nut loaf and mushrooms for dinner later that night. He also got some bread made and baked for lunch. There was a little of Joel's cheese left over and honey from Olif's hives. So it was going to be a good lunch.

By the time the pouches were about half done, lunch was ready. The three of them had been so busy that they didn't even notice that Olif had left. When he called them to eat, they were surprised.

Kali had been curled up, sleeping in her corner. At least *she* thought of it as her corner.

Everyone put down their projects and went with Olif. They went outside to where the fire was. It was well in sight of the portal field, as was everything around the farm.

The sun was warm, with a pale blue light. The trees were in full leaf; some had beautiful flowers of pink and purple that had the most wonderful smell. They were all filling the air with a sweet, light smell. That tree was called a Mellow Wane tree because the smell made you feel peaceful and content. Sen and Seth had seen them before when they had gone on trips with their families. Never had they seen so many together or felt the effect of them.

There was a table by the fire and they all grabbed the vegetable kabobs and spread them over the grate to roast. Then they all got some salad and warm bread to start with. They were hungrier than they had realized and ate a lot of salad before the vegetables were done roasting. They continued their conversation from the craft room, which had to do with what they had found and what they were making.

Miranda had used the pendant that her great grandfather had made as part of a clasp to keep things safe in the pouch. One side of the pouch looked very plain, except for the material. The other side had a special cut-out for the feather of light to stay in. It also had a little flap to protect it when it was not being used. That way, if it needed to absorb light or be used, it could, without having to be removed from the pouch.

Seth and Sen had liked the basic design so much that they copied it. They each put their own unique touches to their pouches with things that they thought would be good for them. Seth had found what looked like a dragon claw, but wasn't as big as one, and it seemed very strong and very sharp. He used it as his clasp. Sen found a button that looked very old, made from gold, that had a rainbow on it and shimmered in the light. He had really liked it and decided to use it.

They had spent most of the time poking around the room and found all sorts of exciting and wondrous things. Miranda only had to finish her strap, which she was going to braid. Sen had found a thin rope that was soft and flexible that he was going to use. Seth was going to use some thick thread that he was going to weave into a small, belt-like strap.

After they all ate and helped clean up, they went back to the craft room and finished their pouches. Then they all went to find Olif, who was getting things together for breakfast the next morning, to show him what their pouches looked like. The feathers were all nicely tucked into the pouches and there was space for other things, should they come to them. Each person was very proud of their handywork and had to show everyone what they had made.

Chapter 10

By then, the two moons were coming up and the stars were twinkling through the darkness. The dragon egg was glowing gently on the roof of the house, all seemed peaceful. Then the lights came, first one then another and another, until the whole farm was full of them. Seth could feel them tugging on him and whispering to them. Miranda was feeling it, too. Sen only could see them. Kali was running around chasing them and Miranda had to call her back and make her go into the cottage so the lights wouldn't take her.

Metuluso came strolling over to them and looked at Sen, and said something to him that turned him sheet-white. It was what most people would call dragon humor. Metuluso told Miranda that she wanted to take Sen up to look at the lights from above. He seemed scared, so Metuluso wanted to know if all three of them wanted to go. Olif thought it was a good idea for them to see it, so they all clamored on top of the dragon. As they launched up, the lights swirled around them, singing their enchanting song and whispering to them. Miranda was a little nervous about the lights and the boys were, too.

Nobody wanted to be taken by the lights. Up they soared, and in a second they were above the lights and the cottage with its glowing light. It was all quite beautiful.

One light had followed them up and was staying with them. Their feathers started to vibrate within the pouches with the swirling of the light and soon the feathers and the light all connected as if they were feeding off each other. This was something new that none of them had ever seen before. Olif had mentioned that something like this happened but he never mentioned that the feathers would connect with the orbs of light. Mituliso was as fascinated as the children were at this interaction between the lights and the feathers.

As the feathers of light grew brighter, so did the orb of light. Everything became very bright; then Metuluso shot up higher like a rocket, and the light from the feathers attached lines of light to the orb of light. Then the orb broke off into three smaller lights and danced with the feathers till they grew bigger and took off on their own. They all stared at the feathers, as they took on a new glow. They had thought that they were shiny before, but now they shimmered with a new radiance, one that made you want to become one with the light.

The lights were far below and swarmed around the field with the portal. More and more were coming, and you could see the twinkles coming through the woods. Then, all of a sudden, the portal opened and out stepped a dragon of light.

They could see Olif greeting the dragon. The lights were a flurry of activity, and then they all extended beams of light to the dragon and the dragon to them. The light became blinding and the song that rose up to them was enchanting and enticing, even to Metuluso. She fought the urge to fly down into the middle of it all.

Then, when they thought they couldn't stand it anymore, it was over and the lights faded back into the forest. The light dragon stood there with Olif for a minute then looked right up at the four of them and he keened to them in a sweet, lonely voice.

Metuluso couldn't resist and down they came. She landed right in front of the light dragon, very gracefully. She didn't want to look foolish in front of him. He was much larger than her, *and his eyes,* she thought, *oh his eyes.* None of them had ever seen eyes like that. They looked like they held the universe in them.

The children tumbled off Metuluso. They didn't land as gracefully as she had, and Olif just looked amused. The dragon of light gave each one of them a long, searching look. Then gave Metuluso a nod and they walked off into the field, one glowing like a small sun and the other dark in comparison.

Olif looked at the three of them and just started to laugh and laugh. He was laughing so hard that tears were streaming down his face. All he said was, "You all looked so funny, falling off the dragon and trying to be so serious; now you look so confused. This is what a typical day in the life of a portal keeper is like. I know you thought, 'Oh, poor old Olif living out here all alone with nobody to talk to.' But as you can see, my life is very fascinating and, when I get a dull moment, I'm very grateful."

Everyone had forgotten about poor Kali locked up in the house, but she was now barking up a storm and wanting out. It was safe for her to be outside, now that the lights had all gone off to wherever they go. As soon as they opened the door, she raced out to see what she had missed. Like an arrow, she headed straight to the two dragons in the field, not even looking at Miranda. Miranda was slightly insulted, but she quickly got over it.

The three children were talking about what an eventful first day they had had at the portal keeper's house. The boys were in shock and awe at what had happened to them, and Miranda was surprised too. Things had happened to them that they hadn't even dreamed about because they didn't even know that they existed.

All the stuff that had happened made them hungry, but they weren't tired at all as they had lots to say to each other about their own unique experience with the dragon.

It seemed that he had touched each of their minds. He had not intruded into their thoughts like Metuluso had done to Sen, but he had just touched each one with a greeting, touching each one with a love that had left them both dazzled and overwhelmed. From that love, which was shared with each one of them, they now had so much energy that they were just buzzing all over the place. Olif explained to them that the dragon of light takes the light and turns it to pure energy, then he takes a little tiny bit and gives it to each of them.

Sen looked at his feather and just about fell off the bench he was sitting on.

He had been listening to the others, but had gotten distracted and was fiddling with the pouch when he turned it over and saw the feather was like a little sun or star glowing. It had absorbed so much energy from the balls of light that it looked like it was about to explode from the porch—it almost blinded him to look at it.

Seth and Miranda looked at their feathers, and, as their lights turned towards each other, they connected in bright lines of color, forming a triangle. In the center was a ball of pure energy. It looked like a swirling mass of light with a hole in the middle. Olif told them that they had just formed a mini-vortex that light energy could come through, and later they would learn what to do with it. But now they needed to eat and ground themselves or they would be up for days running around like Kali in maniacal joy.

They ate roasted eggplant and peppers with cheese and two loaves of bread. After they had eaten, everyone got really sleepy all at once and Olif told them to all go off to bed. Even Kali was dragging her feet too, which was not at all like her. As they headed for the house, from the outdoor kitchen, the stars twinkled in the sky, and the two moons hung there as if waiting for something else to happen, but all was quiet.

Once in their rooms, everyone was curled up and asleep in a twinkle of an eye.

Olif went back outside and met up with the two dragons, who were talking in the field since neither one had ever met a dragon from another dimension before. They found it very unusual to say the least. Metuluso was fascinated by him, and he was fascinated by her. His rainbow lights kept shifting, as her eyes kept shifting color. His name was Tibaru and he was one of the elders. He came through the gate about every two weeks or so to exchange energy from the lights. That's how both the lights and beings from the dimension of light survived. It is an exchange of energy with other dimensions that gives and brings life to them. That's why the feathers that fell off the bird glowed as the lights surrounded them. It was that exact exchange that brings life to all dimensions.

Tibaru told Metuluso that each dragon of light had a portal into another dimension that was their responsibility. They were to take care of the lights, which connect the dimensions together. For both the dragons and the balls of light to survive, they needed to take in the life energy of each other's dimensions in an energy exchange between dimensions. Each dragon, when given a portal, became dependent on the lights of that dimension. So it was an equal trade, and it had been that way from the beginning, as far as anyone knew.

Metuluso had wanted to know why her dragon friends had never seen one of them.

He explained that they come to portals in remote areas and don't go far from them. If they stayed too long in another dimension, they would die. So only the keepers of the portals ever got to see them and knew of them. These light dragons held the key to portal travel. They were the only beings who could entirely and innately control where they went. All other travel was random, except for the portal keepers, who could control it to a certain extent. Tibaru told Metuluso that he would try to teach her how to travel to the dimensions she wanted to go to. He didn't know if she could but he had hope that they were enough alike that she could do it.

The three of them talked into the small hours of the morning. As the moons began to set and the light of day came, Tibaru had to leave.

They strolled over to the portal. As they got closer, the portal began to glow as it appeared and Tibaru walked through, leaving Olif and Metuluso in the silence of the morning. Then the birds woke with a blast of happy chirping and they both were content.

Chapter 11

Back in the village, everyone was all a-twitter. The children had been gone only a day, but everyone was already missing them. Seth's and Sen's parents were ready for them to come home. They were worried about their children riding off on a dragon's back, even though there was a deeper knowing that they would be safe. Olif also seemed like a nice enough man, but nobody knew him very well.

Little Miranda, she was so sweet, everyone had fallen in love with her and she seemed to have knowledge of the dragon who seemed to be her guardian. That put Joel and Myella's mind at rest somewhat. They all really missed their boys, even though they had only been gone one day.

Fern was sad, of course; she had wanted to be a part of the adventure, but she got stuck taking care of her sisters and brothers. As she was milking the goats, she was thinking how much fun it would've been to get to go on the dragon and fly away. She decided right then that she would volunteer to watch for what the wind blew in. She hadn't had much interest before, but now ...

So tonight, she decided, would be the night for her first watch. She just had to get permission from her parents, which may not be as easy as she would hope, but she was determined.

She went to the village elder who was in charge of the watch, and told him that she would like to become a watcher now that Seth and Sen were gone. The elder whose name was Witcha, looked at her for an uncomfortable minute, just as though he was looking through her.

Then he asked, "Do you hear the lights?"

She said, "No."

Witcha then asked, "Do you fear the lights?"

Again she answered, "No." She really didn't care much one way or the other about the lights. She just thought they had always been and will always be.

Witcha liked her answers. She seemed like a very level-headed girl who wouldn't be all scared if something strange blew in, and he *did* need new watchers.

That's how Fern got her new job and finally got out of watching her brothers and sisters. She went home to tell her parents. At first, they were worried about her out there all alone at night, but she told them that Sal, Seth's older brother, would be there too.

They felt much better about that. Sal was a very responsible and practical boy who would never let anything happen to anyone if he could help it. So it was with both parents' "blessings" that Fern went on her first watch.

As night approached, Sal went to Fern's house to get her and they walked towards the field where the lights were. Fern had a bag of snacks and a blanket. She was a little nervous, but with Sal there it felt safe.

Her first night was very uneventful.

There wasn't even one light anywhere to be seen and not even the tiniest of breezes. The two moons hung in the sky, full of the blue light of the sun, and the stars twinkled all night, and the weather was mild. Altogether, it was a perfect evening, only a little dull for Fern. Both Fern and Sal were disappointed that nothing big and exciting happened that night. After the last couple of days, they were hoping for some more excitement. Instead, they had a very pleasant conversation that night.

The next morning, the village was glad to hear things were back to normal. Fern went back home to bed somewhat disappointed, but glad her first night was easy. Sal and Fern had the rest of the week together, then she would be on her own. They would rotate between four of them, with five days on and fifteen days off. That way, nobody got stuck with too much and nobody's family suffered too much. It was nice for Fern not to have to do chores or take care of little ones. She wondered why she hadn't wanted to do it before as she drifted off to sleep.

Life quickly got back to normal, after all the excitement of the past few days. The winds hadn't blown in anything new and things were going well for everyone.

Fern woke up mid-afternoon. She had missed all the morning chores, and she didn't even feel guilty. She got up and wandered into the kitchen to see what there was for food, and found her mom starting to get dinner ready and finishing up a batch of cheese. They had some of the best goats in the village, and the milk they got was creamy and delicious. All the excess was made into cheese that was traded with the merchants who came through on their travels.

Fern's mom was always pleasant and had a good sense of humor, traits that one of Fern's little sister's, Ella, had gotten. Ella was friends with Swela, and was the funniest little thing. Ella was helping with getting dinner started and Ella entertained Fern as Fern made a small sandwich of bread, cheese, tomatoes, and cucumbers.

They lived where it was warm all year, so they had fresh vegetables year-round. Some of the plants in their garden were as old as Fern. They just kept producing more food as long as they got fed. The evenings would cool down a little, but it mostly stayed around eighty degrees all the time. The plants loved it there. Her family had one of the biggest gardens in the village, and she loved to spend time in the gazebo that sat in the center of their garden. That's where she took her sandwich to eat.

Their garden had a variety of vegetables, herbs, and fruit, along with various flowers, all arranged attractively.

There wasn't much for her to do but sit quietly and eat her sandwich, which she was very happy about. She got to rest and look at the garden that she loved.

She had spent most of her life out here with the plants, and the plants seemed to respond well to her touch. She even had a special place for the "weeds" to grow. When a big storm came in, she was always there to get everything protected. When it was time to harvest the food, she always knew which vegetables or fruits were ready to pick and which ones needed just one more day.

While she was sitting and enjoying the day and the food, she started to wonder how they had come to live in this place. It seemed so perfect and peaceful. Everyone had taken for granted that they had always been here. The other villages around thought the same thing, but someone somewhere had to know. So she decided to go and ask her Mom. They had a great relationship and could talk about everything; she even shared her feelings about Seth with her Mom.

In the kitchen, her little sister had started to make honey cookies, her favorite. Fern and her Mom started talking about what it had been like watching for the lights the night before. Fern was surprised that there were no lights or wind. Her mom was glad that Sal had been there to talk to. Her mom worried about her daughter being out there alone all night.

Fern had grabbed some potatoes while she was in the garden and was going to make some potato salad for the watch that night, along with some cheese and bread. They had made sun tea that had been brewed all day long and was ready to be cooled off. As night came, it would be refreshing to have the tea.

As she was making her late-night snack and chatting with her Mom, she asked how they had all come to live in such a great place. Her mother was surprised with the question—everyone was so content that nobody ever even thought about it.

She thought that it had been by accident that they had discovered this place. Then, when the lights took the people, everyone had just decided to stay so that when the people came back the rest of the village would still be there. It had turned out to be a good place, with other villages around them who seemed content, too. Everything they needed was there and as long as there was a watcher, things were good.

The village had grown since the people were taken. Families had grown and there was little sickness. Maybe the occasional cold or broken bone or cut something, but generally people lived to be about one hundred and fifty years old and they usually died in their sleep. By the time they stopped talking, it was time for Fern to go on her watch with Sal.

He was walking down the path to get her when she looked out the window, so she quickly gathered up her things and was ready to take off when he arrived. This time, she had her spindle with her and a bag of cotton to spin while they watched.

As evening approached and the sun went down, there were streaks of green running through the sky. It was beautiful. They had a great view as the stars started to come out and the moons came up, which were starting to wane now.

Fern pulled her spinning out once they settled in, and Sal took out his knife and started carving. They both had thought to bring something to keep themselves busy. They were talking and working on their projects when the lights started to drift in. First one, then the next and the next, until there were lights everywhere. Sal couldn't hear them and neither could Fern. That made them good watchers, since there was no threat to them.

The lights came and danced around them, weaving a hypnotic spell. It was enchanting to watch as the lights' colors changed. They both stopped their work and their conversation to try to hear what the lights were saying, but they heard nothing.

Chapter 12

Meanwhile, Seth, Sen, Miranda, and Kali were already going to sleep after a particularly hard day again. Their lives were just the opposite of calm. When they woke up, Olif had plans for them. First was to meditate with each of their feathers to get in touch with them.

Surprisingly, Sen was the best at that. With all the dragon language he had gotten the day before, he quickly quieted his mind and slipped right into communication with his feather.

As the three of them sat in a triangle, the feathers linked, and a ball of light appeared.

Olif started to show them some basic things they could do with the light: they could make it hot or cold, or start a fire, or keep the light visible to guide you. They could dim it or brighten it, too. There were so many things they could do with the feathers to keep them busy.

After a few hours of practice, they were getting tired, and Olif gave them a break. They were pretty excited about their accomplishments and were chattering about, "I did this, did you see?" and, "Did you see me do that?" between mouthfuls of bread and honey that had the most delicate taste of flowers. Olif said it came from an island in a dimension that had a yellow sun, which was about all he knew about that dimension.

After a short rest, they were ready to get back to work, but this time they were going on a hike. To do the task they were to be sent on, they also had to be in good shape and be able to work together and think together. Kali got to go on this trip and so did Metuluso.

Seth was going to have to learn to link with everyone. The others already knew how. Kali just slipped into their minds with all her wild doggie thoughts of, "what is this smell—and that smell," and, "oh look a stick," which made everyone laugh.

After a few minutes of Seth trying to link, Metuluso linked with him the same way he had linked with Sen. That surprised him, but he was aware of what was happening because Sen had described it to him yesterday, so it wasn't a really big shock. It was very odd to have all that information downloaded in his brain so quickly. He had to sort out all the thoughts that were his from the thoughts of the others. As things cleared, he could "hear" the thoughts of each being that he was linked to. Even Kali, who was having a great time, of course.

They started out on their hike, with Metuluso flying ahead as a scout and Kali checking for anything on the ground. She had suddenly become serious and focused, and very protective of everyone in the party. Olif took the lead because this was their first hike and he knew the area.

As they walked through the woods, they saw big trees that were twenty feet across the base of the trunk, and which must have been at least one thousand years old. As they came to a clearing in the center of the trees, Olif said Metuluso had left to get some food. She hadn't eaten for a few days and needed to hunt.

Olif then had everyone sit in a circle and explained to them how to listen to the trees. They had to still their minds, then reach out to the trees with their minds. It was like projecting a beam of light with their feathers. As they did it, they started to feel the connection to the trees. The trees started to whisper in their minds like the lights did, except it was a slow methodical whisper, not like the lights that were a faster, more frenzied whisper. Both were fascinating to the children.

As the trees whispered, the children realized that the trees were talking among themselves and didn't even notice that the children were there. They couldn't understand the trees, but felt a great comfort from them. Even Kali had calmed down and was lying next to Miranda with her head on her feet.

After a while, Miranda and the boys withdrew from the trees with a feeling of contentment. Olif had already withdrawn and was waiting. He asked if anyone had learned anything, but no one could think of any words. He said they would try again later, but it was a good start.

Sen was able to hear the trees and the lights songs now that Metuluso had linked ith him. He wasn't even scared of the light's songs any more with the dragon knowledge he possessed now he was able to control his feelings of fear all though he still got wildly happy and excited.

Miranda was happy and Kali was content as they started on their hike again. Sen and Seth joked with each other as they took off, all following Olif, as he wound through the paths of the forest.

When the sun started to drop, Olif said it was time to go home. He couldn't be away from the portal for too long. They started on their way home. He took them through some shortcuts, and before they knew it, they walked into the field where the portal was. Metuluso was in the field, waiting for them.

Olif had sent her to guard the portal after she had eaten. That way, he could concentrate on their lesson. As they approached, she greeted them. She was in a very good mood and so was everyone else. Metuluso had had a good time flying and hunting, the group's lesson had gone well, for the first attempt. Olif had taught each of them to connect with the trees. Miranda and Kali had blended well with Seth and Sen. The trees even seemed content with the first attempt. There was a lot more to learn, it seemed, than just going off to find the lost people.

As the days passed, everyone started to work as a team and to think as one. They learned to feel the earth's rhythm and see the life energy coming off of everything. The lights would come and dance and sing around them. They would pull out their feathers and connect to the lights. Tibaru came to visit and to exchange energy with the lights a couple of times, and stayed long enough to teach them new ways of communicating with the lights.

The lights no longer were frightening to them; the children welcomed the lights as friends. Some lights even had personalities. It was surprising to the five of them and Olif that the lights had personalities. The lights would send messages back and forth to Miranda's parents. Sometimes she would even get a little care package from her parents with something special for her, which she would share with the others. That was a very special treat. Her parents were very proud of her for being chosen for this quest, and a little sad because their baby was becoming an adult.

Chapter 13

One day, Seth said he needed to go home and check on something. Nobody even questioned it; they all knew from being so connected from practicing with the feathers.

So Metuluso took him to his house where his Mother was worried sick about him. She was overjoyed to see he was okay. One of his brothers had gotten hurt and they didn't know if he would be alright or not. Seth looked at him with his broken leg that he had gotten from messing around on the stones at the lake.

Seth then took out his feather and called the lights. His family became afraid except for Swela—she had been blessed by Metuluso, so she liked the lights. Then the lights connected to each other through the feather and encircled Seth and his brother. As Seth was telling Quinn to not be scared, the light began to change colors and Quinn's leg started to heal. The black color started to turn pink as circulation came back to the leg.

After that was done, the whole village gathered at Seth's house to learn what had happened. They had seen the dragon come and were all curious to know if they had found the people yet. Seth had lots of talking to do.

While he was telling everyone what had happened to him and Sen, Swela slipped away to find Metuluso. She had fallen in love with the dragon, and now was her chance to see Metuluso all by herself.

The villagers were very excited to see Seth, and they had a million questions for him. Seth was very polite and answered as many questions as he could without startling everyone.

Swela was so happy to be forgotten, and be alone with the dragon. She just loved those eyes full of swirling colors. Metuluso put her head down and nuzzled Swela with her nose, which made her giggle, then Metuluso looked straight into her eyes and told her to climb on her back.

She put a leg out for Swela to climb on her back. Swela scampered up on the dragon's back and sat there patting the pretty scales. That felt very comforting to both her and the dragon. Metuluso hadn't felt anything like that for a long time.

Swela just sat there on her back for a very long time, chatting about all sorts of things.

Metuluso found her voice soothing and it was nice to be quiet with the little girl on her back.

The fields were turning golden, and the next crop of vegetables were getting ready to plant. The gardens looked lush and well tended. The goats were all fat and happy and didn't even seem to mind Metuluso sharing their field.

Ty and Joel walked up to this peaceful scene and were surprised to see their daughter on a drowsy dragon's back, chatting away. It was quite the scene. They asked Swela what she was doing and she announced that she was going to be a dragon rider when she grew up just like Miranda. She said she was protecting Metuluso right now.

Metuluso gave Ty and Joel a wink, which surprised them. Those swirling golden eyes were so mesmerizing that they got caught up in them, and it was Joel who broke away from them first. She asked Swela if she wanted to eat with everyone.

A big pot luck had just been thrown together so everyone could hear what was happening at Olif's. Swela wasn't at all interested; she wanted to stay with the dragon. Ty asked Metuluso if it was ok and to his surprise he got a clear "yes" in his mind. His eyes flew wide open and Metuluso winked again. Joel asked what had just happened and he started telling her as they were walking back to the house. Swela just smiled with contentment as they left.

Seth was careful answering questions. He didn't want the whole village to come out to Olif's house and he only told them things that they could understand. He noticed how much he had changed in just the few weeks he had been gone. He loved all the people of the village he was raised in, but he knew he could never go back to that life.

He could now see a halo of the colors around the village people and knew who would be getting sick and who was healthy.

After everyone had a good visit, and had left, Fern was still there. She seemed happy to see him and Seth was certainly happy to see her. They took off on a little walk to catch up on news, and Seth was surprised to hear that she had become a watcher. He wanted to know if the wind had blown anything in.

She said, "No, not lately." Nothing really appeared during her watches. She said the lights danced for her, and sometimes she thought that they may have been whispering to her, but there was no way she was going to go to them. She didn't want to be blown away.

That was the good old practical Fern that he loved.

They had a good visit, and he told her to try to listen to lights. He said he would send her messages through the lights, and that he could now understand the lights. If there was need in the village, he would know by the lights telling him.

He knew there would be no need because nothing ever happened in their little village. Everything was good.

They said goodbye as she went off for her watch, and Seth went to say goodbye to his family. Seth knew he would have to pry Swela off the dragon so they could leave.

He was right. Swela put up a fuss and cried, but Metuluso told her she would take her for a ride next time she came if she was a very good girl. That did it, she was down in a flash, giving the dragon kisses on the nose.

Everyone laughed as Seth told them what had just happened. Then he was up on the dragon's back, and they took off, but not without a large package of everything his and Sen's mothers could think of to send with him.

The flight back seemed short, and Seth was glad to get back. Sen was excited to get treats from home, and Olif was glad they could get back to work. Tomorrow was a big day—they would go through the portal for the first time! Olif wanted everyone rested and ready to go.

Chapter 14

They had been learning that each portal has a different signature and how to find it. None of them had actually done it, but they had been told how to find it.

Every portal like theirs had a keeper who watched it and monitored it to see what came through. Olif had made arrangements for the group's first trip to Miranda's home. All five of them would go together as a team. The portal keeper would be there to greet them and help. Things were all set for leaving first thing in the morning.

They all went to bed early—tomorrow would be a big day. With lots happening in the morning, it would get busy, so everyone had to be well rested and organized before going through the portal. They would be gone a day and a night, then return the next day. Miranda's parents had been told and would be waiting for her. A few of the lights would be going, too.

When morning arrived, everyone was up and ready to go. They were a little apprehensive because none of them believed that you could control where you went. They were, however, willing to trust Olif.

They were up and had a quick breakfast—nothing heavy. Olif had warned them that stepping through the portal would make them queasy, and Miranda had said that, when she had been blown there, she had felt queasy and confused. Olif told her that between was a little different because the winds will also make people confused.

Olif and everyone went out to the field and he opened the portal. As it opened, there were many colors that swirled by, and each color was a different dimension. Olif only knew thirteen of them, while the others were unknown to him. He stopped the portal at a beautiful sky-blue color that almost matched Miranda's skin. Nobody knew how he had stopped it.

A face appeared on the other side. Olif and the other person, who looked a lot like Miranda, talked a few minutes.

Then Olif turned to the children and said, "Time to go."

Everything was ready and Metuluso went first, then Miranda and Kali. Sen and Seth went together.

As they stepped in, Miranda felt a blast of icy cold and then hot and then she was back in her own world. The boys felt the same thing, only they were now in a new, strange world.

There was Kali, racing about and jumping all over everyone, from friends she had not seen for a while to friends that had just come with her. Miranda's parents were waiting for her by the portal.

Miranda ran to them and gave them both the biggest hug you could imagine.

The boys just stared. Things looked the same, but also different somehow. There were trees around a big field and they were standing in the middle of the field. There was a cottage and a barn there, also. Another dragon was waiting in the field, as well. This one's skin was more of a greenish gold color and his eyes were a deep emerald green that swirled around. He was Metuluso's mate and his name was Fresalos.

Miranda's parents were almost as tall as Seth. They came up to his chest. They both had pale blue skin and long silver hair and their names were Tulsa and Emily. They looked ageless, just like Miranda, and they wore clothes made out of the same shimmery fabric that Miranda's clothes were made from. Tulsa had a tunic on and pants that flowed in the breeze. Emily wore a dress that clung to her body and a cape that changed colors as she moved. It was hard to tell where she was. She almost seemed invisible.

Metuluso had missed her home, and Miranda was a-whirl with chatter to her parents, so that left Seth and Sen just standing there looking around. Petrous, who was the gatekeeper of this dimension, came up to talk to them.

He introduced himself and he showed them some of the things from his world. They were similar, yet different: the colors seemed just a bit off, and, when they looked at the sun, it wasn't pale blue here—it was white. That was what the difference was.

Petrous told them that most things were the same from dimension to dimension, but some things were quite different.

Each dimension had its own kind of people. He himself wasn't much taller than Miranda, and he had a tunic with long flowing sleeves that tied at the wrist, with a belt at the waist and tight pants with boots up to his knee made out of something the boys had never seen. It looked soft, but it was also very strong. They both were envious of those boots.

After a few minutes, Petrous asked if everyone would like to come inside for something to eat and drink.

His house was a lot like Olif's house. He had one of the dragon eggshell lights in his ceiling, too, and he had lots of rooms with big windows in them and lots of unusual things in the house. His house was rounder with a lot of intricate carvings around the doors and ceiling.

He told them that he had lots of time to do things. He explained that he had been a portal keeper for over two thousand years. The last keeper had passed on to the realm of pure light after four thousand years. Some of the things in the house were that old, but most of the things had been replaced. Even the walls had been rebuilt.

Seth and Sen couldn't really conceive of anyone living that long. They asked Miranda's parents how old they were. They answered three thousand and two years and three thousand and fifty years.

Petrous explained how time worked differently in each dimension. Even though they are all on the same planet, time exists differently in each dimension. They all live at the same time, just at different frequencies, so when you pass through a portal, your frequency changes to exist there.

That was why Olif had picked Miranda's dimension. The boys had already begun to pick up Miranda's frequency just by becoming a team with her. Kali was like a chameleon and could adapt to wherever she was. When the winds had blown Miranda to Seth, she had felt queasy and confused because her vibration had to adjust.

Everyone was settling down and the boys wanted to see what kind of food they had in this dimension. They were surprised that it was very similar to their own food. Petrous had fruit that looked almost like theirs. He had put out some pears, plums and grapes, along with cheese and bread. It tasted just as good as any of the cheese and bread at home. Petrous said that eating any food of that dimension changed their vibration even more. The water here was so sweet you didn't even want to drink anything else.

Chapter 15

After a while, Miranda wanted to go home. She also wanted the boys to see the ocean. She knew they had never seen an ocean and they really wanted to see one. Petrous didn't want them wandering around too much, for fear someone might see them and be frightened of their brown skin and their size, as they were giants compared to Miranda's people.

Metuluso volunteered to take them to the ocean where the dragons lived and where no people visited so they could be safe. The portal had to remain secret from most people. The only reason Miranda's parents knew of this portal was because the winds had blown her away.

The ride to the ocean was fun and exciting. They had a great view and got to see the town from a distance. It had great towers that spiraled up to the heavens and huge trees that were homes to some of the elves.

The town was old—they could feel the ancientness of the city. Not a whole lot had happened there in a very long time to make things very exciting. It was a golden age of peace for them, and their art and culture flourished during this time. There had been a time before they had crossed to this dimension that there had been wars between them and the evil from other planes of existence.

The portal keepers were so important because they kept evil from crossing into their planes of existence. Not very many people knew of these guardians, whose jobs were to protect them. The portal keepers all knew each other and would speak through the portals and send things to each other. They could not pass through to another dimension for trade or go visit, for then their portal would be unprotected.

Petrous had been a perfect host, with all sorts of goodies and special treats that he had exchanged with other portal keepers from other plains. They would pass them through the portals with each other, like they did when sending Miranda her care packages. One treat that the boys really liked was a roll of chopped nuts mixed with honey and butter, which was really good. They had fruit juice with ice in it. They had never had ice or even seen ice before.

The flight to the ocean was breath taking to the boys. As they soared over Miranda's town they were mesmerized by the magnificence of the buildings and the size of the town. They had never seen anyplace that large where people lived (or elves). Their only thing to compared to was there little village.

The flight to the ocean was all that Miranda had described to them with the mountains and cliffs.

Sen and Seth had never seen an ocean before, so even the smell of salt air was new to them. They were very excited about how blue it was and how the waves washed on the shore. As they looked out on to the sun setting and the deep pinks and oranges in the sky, they knew this was a whole new world to them.

They found some beautiful shells on the beach and waded in the ocean. There were dragons playing on the shore and they swam in the waves. It all seemed so peaceful and surreal at the same time. The sand was pearl white and so fine it felt like silk on your feet. They didn't want to leave.

Metuluso came up to them and told them it was time to go back to Petrous's house. She had already said her goodbyes to many an envious dragon, for she got to go on an adventure.

Sen and Seth learned a lot of new things while they were at Petrous's house and had a great visit with him. He told them about a different dimension he knew about. There even were rumors about one dimension that an entire village had been blown to. He didn't know which one, he just knew that they were there and seemed to be happy.

He laughed as he told them about the portal keepers' gossip hotline which went portal by portal so each one of them would know what was going on out there. Also, they sometimes just liked each other's company.

He knew of about twenty dimensions, which was more than Olif knew about. He even wrote them down for Olif to look at. He told them that would help.

Miranda was at home visiting her family. While her visit was to be secret from her friends until the adventure was over, her parents savored every minute they got to spend with her. She had her favorite meal of roasted eggplant with a spicy curry sauce and sweet rice, and for dessert there were mangos—lots of mangos. She ate until she couldn't eat any more.

Kali was happy to be home and curled up in her bed. The star on her head was glowing and she was content. Miranda stayed up visiting with her parents until dawn, when it was time to go back to the portal. Metuluso came and got them as they were stepping onto the balcony. All three of them hopped on her back and off they went.

There was only one set of eyes that had seen Miranda come and go by dragon with Kali. And those weren't friendly eyes. There were a few elves that were filled with jealousy and always looking to cause trouble Lagos was one of them. He was very unhappy and always trying to create trouble. Which he now thought he could do. But that is another story for another time.

Everyone met back at the portal. Then everyone said goodbye and the portal opened and they could see Olif waiting for them on the other side. First in jumped Kali, then the rest followed, with Metuluso last, carrying a big basket from Miranda's parents. It had clothes for her and some of her favorite foods, with lots of mangos and some sweet bread that her mother had made for her.

Olif was happy to have them back.

He had missed them, even though they were only gone a day. He had been alone for so many years that having them live with him was a real treat. It was unexpected to him how much he was getting attached to them; he hadn't realized how much till they were gone. Miranda ran up to Olif and gave him a big hug. The boys also gave him big hugs as well. They were so happy to see him too. Olif got this strange feeling, one that he hadn't felt since he was a child, one of feeling loved. He almost started to cry from happiness but he pulled himself together and became Olif the portal keeper but changed just a bit. Then they all went into the house to talk about the experience.

Seth showed him the list that Petrous had given him. As he looked at it, he nodded in agreement. There were many other dimensions, but some could only be accessed at certain times. These were the closed dimensions, the ones none of the portal keepers knew much about. Miranda had a great idea about asking the lights where these dimensions were. Otherwise, they could be searching a very long time for the missing people. Olif thought it was a good idea to try.

Just then, the portal opened and out walked Tibaru. Everyone went outside to greet the dragon of light and to ask if he would mind asking the lights while they were exchanging energy, about the lost people. Tibaru thought that was a good idea also. He knew where the people were but it was their quest and they had to figure out where the lost people were. As the lights came to feed with the dragon by exchanging energies, there was a hum of excitement that hadn't been seen before. Then all the lights just took off and vanished.

Tibaru said the lights were searching; some had heard about the lost people and some hadn't, but they would all search. Some said they remembered when they had come to dance with the people and the wind had blown them away, but none knew where they were blown to. The lights were sorry that the wind had blown them away because then nobody would dance with them anymore and the village people were afraid of them.

The lights said it was the wind that was to be feared, not them. Tibaru said he would talk to the other dragons of light to see if any of them could find anything out. All the dragons in his realm went to different dimensions to exchange energy with the lights. So now it was a matter of waiting to find out if anyone knew of anything.

Tibaru stayed and visited with Metuluso a while after the lights had left. He glowed a white light with little rainbows twinkling in his skin. It was beautiful to look at him. As the night got deeper and the stars shined, he got brighter. The two dragons were across the field talking and all the children could do was stare at them. The light from Tibaru reflected off of Metuluso's blue-green skin. Together they looked like blue and white rainbows with the light from the moons shimmered off of them.

Olif took everyone inside and they talked about what it was like to pass through the portal and Miranda compared it to how it was when the wind had blown her there. She said the portal was quicker and you didn't get so mixed up. She definitely liked portal travel better: you could see where you were going and what was on the other side. She liked that about it.

The boys didn't have anything to compare it to. They just thought it was fantastic to go from one dimension to the next. They were anxious to go see what another dimension was like. Olif tried to tell them not to be so eager, that they all weren't so friendly and some were downright scary. The boys listened to him and agreed to wait.

They had a big meal with lots of salad and a noodle soup with bread to sop the juice up. For dessert, Miranda brought out a box her mother had sent with her, that had one of her favorite desserts in it. It looked like stars with crystal sugar coating on them, that looked like they were twinkling, and it had just the slightest taste of honeysuckle when you bit into it. She said it was one of her favorites. Everyone said that they could see why she liked it so much.

Everyone was tired after the day and nobody had gotten any sleep the night before, so with full bellies they all headed off to bed.

Chapter 16

Sometime during the night was when it happened.

Fern was watching the fields and Olif was at his house getting things set for the night when things came crashing down. Fern heard a loud yowl and jumped almost out of her skin as the winds all of a sudden picked up. Olif ran from the house to see fire in the sky and Kali, Miranda, Sen, and Seth flew from their beds.

As soon as they were awake they could tell something was terribly wrong. They ran out to find Olif and Metuluso and they saw the fire in the sky, too. It was coming from the direction of the village.

Everyone was scared. Tibaru was still with them and Metuluso told the children that they would go and see what was happening.

All the animals were in a panic. Olif was trying to calm them. Miranda put a bubble around the barn and the house to try to calm them which was starting to work when there was another loud clap of noise which sent them into another panic.

Fern was too terror-stricken to move. The field had just split open, fire was coming out of it, the air itself seemed to split. She had never seen or heard of anything like it. All of the village was awake and people and animals were running everywhere.

The fire just stayed in one place. It didn't move, but it looked very big and very scary.

There were big crashes of noise, like two claps of thunder hitting each other. Then the fire parted and two men and one creature, who looked and felt very evil, walked through and out of the flames. They didn't look friendly or feel nice.

Fern fled from her watch spot and went straight to the village. People were scattered all over the place. Fern quickly told everyone what had happened. The men gathered right away to go see who and what was in the field.

They gathered at least twenty men to go to the field. The fire was still burning in the same place and the two men with the creature were just standing there, waiting.

The men were very tall, with long brocaded robes and tall hats that pointed to the sky. They had the creature between them. It was tall, with wings and a bird head and a body like a cat, with a long twitching tail. Its eyes were golden and the creature was black. The villagers were staring at the men, as they stood calmly in the middle of the field.

One of the men raised an arm and then the fire was out.

The other started to talk, but no one could understand him.

Seth's dad stepped forward and told them that nobody could understand them.

The other man was listening and told Seth's father that they knew little of his language, but were able to understand what he was saying.

The villagers could almost understand what was trying to be said.

The strangers said they were explorers who were looking for new lands for their people to come and settle. On the surface, it all seemed friendly enough, but there was *something* not right about these three.

There was a vibration of evil that seemed to be lurking just below the surface.

Ty told them that this land was already taken and he thought it best that they be off looking elsewhere. The men and the creature nodded and walked back toward where the flames had been, as if to leave.

But at the last second they turned and cast flames all over the land. The field began to burn, and as the flames grew. The creature began to howl, a howl that brought everyone to their knees. The flames consumed everything in their path and the villagers were paralyzed. The two men from the flames just laughed a bone-chilling laugh.

Then out of the sky came the dragons, Metuluso flaming in for the kill, and Tibaru right behind, a blazing ball of light so bright the sun looked pale in comparison. The three of them turned to see what was coming, but it was too late. Metuluso's flames fried them in one breath, and as they turned to ashes, the flames disappeared.

The villagers could again move and the people began to run and scream. Some just ran around in circles. Others just collapsed. Nobody knew what to think of the dragons. They had all seen Metuluso before, but not as a fierce fighter, and the dragon of light was something they thought to be feared.

Then, out of nowhere and amid the ashes, sat a statue of pure white light: a perfect dragon baby.

She had delicate white wings and deep purple eyes that penetrated to the depths of the soul. She looked around as if dazed, then looked up at Tibaru and gave a chortle of pure joy.

Then she looked around and spotted Seth's little sister Swela who had run to see what was going on with her father. She chirped one big chirp and ran to her and cuddled up in her arms. Swela was thrilled she was holding a baby dragon.

Tibaru slowly walked up to her and looked into her eyes and saw the love and compassion in her. He knew then that she would be with the baby forever. They had bonded.

As Swela looked at Tibaru, she began to talk to the dragon of light in his own language. He was so stunned that he didn't know how to respond, and he was never caught off guard like that.

She was asking what had happened, and who he was, and where the baby had come from, and who were those awful people.

Her father was just as shocked that his little girl was so bold as to talk to the dragon of light; Metuluso was just proud and beaming at her. She had known about Swela at their first meeting, and she had thought that the little girl would grow up before becoming a dragon partner. But fate had stepped in and put her where she needed to be to save the baby dragon of light.

Tibaru explained to Swela who the bad men were. Swella then turned and told her daddy who the bad men were. They had come from another dimension where they lived in fear and warred to conquer all. They live for the quest and the thrill of the win.

The creature had been a dragon of light that had been captured by the men, who then turned her into an evil being. When Metuluso blasted them with flames, it released her from evil. She then looked around to find a loving soul who would help her mend her wounds. That was Swela, for she loves unconditionally and will be able to mend the broken baby. Now she has to start as a baby again and, as the light grows in her, so will she grow.

Her name was Orrusanu.

She was one of the oldest and wisest of the dragons of light.

"The dragons of light will be glad when she can come back to us", Tibaru explained.

Swela told her daddy all of this, totally oblivious of the entire village listening. By then they all were there, including her mother, who started thinking, "Oh no! Now I have a baby dragon to raise, too!"

Little Orrusanu was curled up, purring in Swela's lap, getting cuddled and patted with a warm light coming out of her body.

The townspeople were all a-chatter about recent events and about wanting things to settle down. They wanted it quiet and calm like before Miranda blew in.

Chapter 17

Meanwhile, Seth, Sen, and Miranda were worried about what was happening in the village. The dragons had flown off quite fast and Olif looked really worried.

At Olif's farm, things were safe and seemed to be settling down. There was no more crashing and rumbling—but then the balls of light came pouring in, thousands of them. Seth had never seen so many and they seemed agitated. Seth could hear them, but couldn't understand what they were saying.

Olif told the children to bring out their feathers, because it was time for another lesson. They looked confused but obeyed.

Olif said to join the feathers like they had practiced. As they did, the jumbled sounds of the balls of light became words.

Miranda and Sen could hear them, too. The sound was clear and musical, like crystals singing. They were mesmerized by it. Their voice was one. They all were saying the same thing at once, so it came out as one voice.

It was a scary thing to hear of the evil men and the bird-cat creature. It became unbelievable as they learned about the dragons and what they did about the baby, and about who became the baby's caretaker. Seth began to laugh and so did Sen because they knew how Seth's mother would take it.

Everyone was relieved about the near-tragedy that was averted thanks to the dragons.

Olif said that he didn't think that they would be coming back because usually people from that dimension won't go back to where their people had been defeated.

Losing their dragon of light is a big loss.

After about two hours, the dragons came back. Tibaru had to go back through the portal.

He told Seth and Olif that Orrusanu would be okay in this dimension while she grew and healed. The orbs of light would protect her. The whole village was there to support her and Swela was thrilled to have her own dragon. She was playing with her when the two dragons left.

Orrusanu was going to have to learn love all over again. Now she had a good home to find it in.

After all the excitement, it seemed time to finally get to bed again. Kali had already gone to Miranda's room and curled up on the bed. The rest of the animals were all back to normal. Tibaru had gone back through the portal and Metuluso was heading to her resting place. Olif was going to keep one eye on the portal.

Everyone went into the main room and sat on the chairs and couches to bask in the light of the eggshell dome. The light gave off a warm glow that slowly released and energized at the same time.

After about an hour everyone was ready for bed. By then it was almost morning, so that day's lessons were to be put off until the next day. Everyone was going to have the day off to catch up on rest.

The next adventure in portal travel was to go to the dimension of light.

Chapter 18

The next day was peaceful. Everyone got a late start, but the chores were eventually done. Kali was back to her old pesky self, wanting everyone to pay attention to her and play chase the stick, which she did for hours. Meals and gardening were all done on time and beds were changed. It was a quite normal day.

The next day, they were all up and ready to go through the portal.

After a quick breakfast of bread and cheese (Seth's Mom had given Metuluso a care package), they were amazed she had had time to do that, what with the new baby dragon that was now part of the family and everything else that had happened that night.

Tibaru had told Swela and her mother how Orrusanu traded energy with the orbs of light. It was very thrilling to them and, as a baby, she needed to trade this energy once a day. So every night they needed to take her out to trade energy. The balls all knew what needed to be done and they would be there to do it.

Tibaru was waiting for the group as they prepared to go through the portal to his world. He wanted to prepare them for what they would see. His world was nothing like theirs. The people and all life forms existed as light. They were solid light.

That sounded strange to the group. Even Olif was a little confused by that.

The dragon told each of them to touch him to feel what they would encounter. He also told them that they couldn't exist long in his world because there was no organic life there.

Everyone felt very honored to touch Tibaru. He was very interesting to feel: he was solid, but also not. His body felt almost like a crystal, but it was flexible to touch, just like the feathers. When you touched it, the rainbows in his body would shimmer and change color. The touch seemed kind of cool but with a strange kind of warmth that was hard to describe.

Tibaru was very patient as each one of them touched him and felt his body. They then asked if that was what his world felt like.

He smiled a big dragon smile and said, "You shall see when we go." The group, being all children, were very excited to get going. All the apprehension had left them as they went to get ready.

Olif had given them packs of food to take and water to drink. There would be nothing for them to eat or drink, as the world they were going to was all light.

As the portal opened, the smiles got bigger as they saw the golden light peek through and felt the peace of that world shine in. Then off they went … first Tibaru, then Metusulo, Kali, Miranda, Seth, and then Sen.

The five of them were so connected now that there was no need for words as they each stepped into the world of rainbow light and crystalline sound. It was a chorus of little tinkling sounds like water chimes and each rainbow had its own distinct sound that blended with the other.

Tibaru had told them that they were one of the few solid-bodied people who ever had entered their world. Nobody said a word—even

Kali was calm. At the other end of the field, there was a crystalline city that they could see.

Here, the portal was not guarded, for only those with a pure heart could enter into this dimension. All the living beings of that world were connected to the source of lights. All thoughts were manifested immediately into the crystal light. It just had to be felt. They didn't need words to express what was needed or required.

As they walked to the City of Crystal Rainbows, balls of light flowed around the five of them as if anxious for information. The spheres of light began to talk excitedly, asking all sorts of questions at once.

The spheres did have a way of communicating to beings that were not of the light by projecting thoughts into the non-light beings. Metuluso was amazed to see everything—not even in her wildest dragon dreams had she imagined this. As she walked, her blue-green body started to take on a golden hue that reflected the rainbows of light. The balls of light began to cover her. As they covered her, she looked like she was becoming a cocoon of light, peace, and love.

Kali was being very calm. She stayed right beside Miranda as they continued their walk to the town with Tibaru. It seemed to take a lifetime to walk that short distance.

As their bodies began to adjust to the dimension, they all began to feel lighter and there was more bounce to their step.

The landscape at first looked like it was all crystal rainbows, but as they adjusted to their surroundings, they started to see all forms of flowers, bugs, birds, lizards—you name it, they saw it all. Each being was made out of light, each thing had its own light, color, and vibration.

As Tibaru walked, the energy that the lights had given him fell off in waves to feed the other life. Seth could see the sheets of energy falling off and for the first time realized how this world existed.

It was truly wondrous!

Everything that was there lived by exchanging energy with each other. The dragons were the exchange conductors. The new energy that the dragons brought in gave life to the whole planet. The dragons also picked up energy from there and stored it to take back to the lights in the other planes. There was an endless supply, exchanged across the dimensions.

The balls of light were everywhere, all chattering away.

As they entered the city, a group of light beings who were the Elders of Light came up to greet them. Tibaru introduced everyone to the Council of Light.

There was Ashtar, who was tall and magnificent in golden light, with long flowing robes of rainbows.

Then there was Tashula. She was of blue light and almost looked like Miranda, with long silvery blue hair that glowed bright then dimmed, almost as if it were breathing. Her robes were of a filmy light, but you couldn't see through them.

Then there was Vaishru, who was of a white light that shone like a sun.

All three of them radiated pure love.

They were magnificent to behold and left the group speechless.

As the introductions were made, each one was given a hug of wonderful pure energy of love washing over and through their bodies. It was as if the universe had just wrapped itself around each of them in a wonderful knowing of love and light and sound. Each hug from each elder left them feeling a little different.

After the introductions, they were brought into the grand chamber where all meetings were held. This room had a very tall podium, a semicircle with tall golden pillars and white walls. The floor was of a white solid light that should have been blinding, but it wasn't.

Tibaru was prepared to talk; he thought it was best for him to begin, since the three children had been speechless for about an hour already.

Kali continued to be extremely calm and obedient.

Metuluso was just as much in awe as everyone else. She had heard of this place but had only believed it was a myth until she had met Tibaru. Now they were all here and it didn't seem real. The council elders had welcomed them but hadn't said much more.

Now was the time to talk.

Vaishru spoke and said that the three of them had been invited as an experiment to see what would happen to them in the realm of light.

Never before had anybody who was not a light being ever entered the realm for more than a few hours.

As light beings, air is not needed, so any physical being would die in a matter of hours. But for this experiment, the lights that traveled the dimensions had brought back air in their light balls, enough to keep them alive for three days.

That would be all the time they had to learn what they needed to know and to leave safely.

Their lessons were to begin immediately and each day they would have a different teacher.

The first was Vaishru.

His task was to teach them the color of sounds. It seemed simple enough but it wasn't at all. Each sound had a color. They had to learn all the colors to match all the sounds. This would let them adjust to each new dimension instantly as they walked into a new dimension. Each dimension had its own set of colors and sounds. By being able to shift to these, they will be able to hop dimensions quite easily.

It took them a little while to get the feeling of it, but with all of the dragon knowledge and Olif's training in meditation, they were picking it up very quickly.

Soon everyone was getting it and it began to be a game. One of them would identify a color, another would match a sound, then Kali would chase it. As they practiced, it started to become second nature and the team of five became a working unit. There were no interruptions to the flow.

Vaishru was very pleasantly surprised. He couldn't believe they fell together so quickly. He could see why they had been put together.

Miranda was so quick at changing vibrations that the boys had trouble keeping up. As they would get tired, the lights would surround them and give them more energy.

Finally, Vaishru said it was time to rest. He knew that they had brought food and water. He took them out to the center of town where there were pillars of light and a light fountain. Then, in the next moment, there appeared a place where they could sit and eat.

It just appeared out of the light.

With a sly smile, Vaishu told them they would learn how to do that tomorrow.

As they sat and ate, they noticed how the food tasted so much better, just like when you are out camping. Olif had put in an extra treat of rose petal candy. He had crystallized the honey somehow, coating the rose petals with it.

They had eaten their cheese and bread for the day. None of them were very hungry because they had gotten all that energy from the lights.

There was a smell of sweet flowers that wafted around them as they sat by the fountain of light.

Kali had found some balls of light and she was getting to know them in her own doggie way. It was wonderful to watch as two such alien life forms got to know each other.

Metuluso was off with Tibaru.

The lights began to take on human appearances. Then some came and started to talk to the children.

The light people had thousands of questions. They told the children that as balls of lights they don't get to see much of the dimensions they are in so everyone was getting questions.

They wanted to know what trees were and what food was. They were very interested to touch it. As balls of light, they had no feeling. But as light beings, they could feel it. For them to feel other things that weren't made from light was very exciting for them. They had no need for food but wanted to see it and feel it.

Some of them took on Kali's shape and found out that playing with her was fun. Those balls got very excited and started to get in the way of the others. Some balls would change form and others would fade in and out.

The dragons and the elders were the only solid light forms that didn't change shape. That was so shocking to Sen, Seth, and Miranda.

They were all spellbound by how the balls of light shifted shape, then appeared solid.

Eventually the group started to get tired. Kali had curled up at Miranda's feet and Sen was yawning.

Vaishru came and took them to the guest quarters that were rarely used, if ever they had been. Once, many years ago, there was a visitor who had come from another dimension to ask for help. Other than that, it was never used.

As they approached the house, it looked like a crystal house with walls of crystal shimmering in the light. Inside there were big soft balls to lay on.

They set down their bags and got some water to drink and then plopped down on the balls. They were so soft and cozy, that they were asleep almost instantly.

Chapter 19

Swela, in the meantime, had her baby light dragon. She never left her for any reason- they were inseparable. When they weren't playing or sleeping, she was holding her and cuddling her. What more could a five year old want then to have her very own baby dragon? Her parents couldn't get her to do anything, but at least she wasn't pestering them about things anymore. The little dragon seemed to adore her. Whenever she was hungry, which seemed to be about twice a day, the balls of light would magically appear, surrounding her. Then the light beams would attach themselves to her along with Swela.

If Swela thought it was wrong, she would start ordering the balls of light around until she thought it was right. The balls of light were very patient with her. There seemed to be an order to the patterns of light and Swela seemed to be aware of it. Orrusanu was like any other baby, not aware of the order. She was captivated by the physical world around her, she wanted to see and feel everything around her. Swela was busy showing her the trees and flowers and the grass. Everything was new and captivating to this little dragon. The house also held many hidden treasures that she was interested in. She grew very fast, almost doubling in size the first day. But she was still cuddly and Swela was so devoted to her and vice versa.

Swela could talk to her in words and she would talk back to her in pictures. After two day's Orrusanu's pictures began to have words. They were in the old dragon language of long ago. She was starting to get dragon memories back. All the dragons of light have all the memories of all dragons. They can't be killed but once in a while they could be captured and turned into a slave for evil, like she had been. Then, when released from the evil, they had to learn what living in love and light was all over again. Orrusanu was lucky to have Swela there to shower her with unconditional love. It was opening her faster than was expected. Swela seemed to know the ancient language quite well as they talked and chirped to each other. All the rest of the family could only watch with contentment as this five year old bonded with a dragon of light.

Seth was the first one to wake up. He laid on the ball of solid light and looked around at the wonders of this world with all the colors of the rainbow and the shimmering in and out of colors. He was truly amazed at how his life had changed. He was just a humble wind/light watcher, with no idea of being the one to find the lost people. Now here he was laying on a bubble of pure light energy in the dimension of light, learning how to identify sounds and colors to go traipsing through dimensions with his best friend and a beautiful little elf. These were the thoughts that went through his mind in the quiet time between awake and sleep.

Just as he was starting to feel overwhelmed, Sen and Miranda woke up along with Kali. Then there was no time for thought. Miranda needed to go to the bathroom, which seemed to be a problem in a dimension of light where there weren't any bathrooms.

She got up and started to explore their shelter. They had been so tired the night before that they all had tumbled into bed and didn't wake up till what they thought was morning, Time here in this dimension ran differently, and being the dimension of light it was, never dark. As she started to look around. A ball of light floated in and changed into a person about the same size as Miranda, only her color kept shifting from blue to purple to red.

She asked Miranda if she needed anything. Miranda explained what she was looking for. The light person brightened a bit then took Miranda down a corridor to a huge bathroom with marble sinks and a huge sunken bathtub. It even had a toilet there.

There was already hot water in the tub which puzzled Miranda. She was wondering where the water came from. Then the light being said, sounding like wind chimes tinkling in the wind, that she would get Miranda's friends so they could bathe together. Miranda had to explain to her that she and the boys didn't bathe together, which puzzled the light being. The balls of light had no feelings of modesty, as they are always exposed in thought and mind to each other.

As Miranda was getting ready to bathe, she noticed how her skin was taking on hues of color and was starting to look transparent. This wasn't upsetting to her at all. She found it rather curious that her skin was starting to take on the colors of the rainbow.

After she finished her bath, she went off to find the boys, who were exploring a huge room full of all sorts of wondrous things. They told Miranda that these things were gifts from all the dimensions, collected by the dragons. It was an archive of cultures from the beginning of time. There was primitive art, wood statues some that were tall and some shorter ones. One that caught his eye was a statue that looked like a griffin, but it was friendly in appearance. It was made of clay and painted in many colors, with decorations in its feathers and around it's head. They all had heard of griffins but none had ever seen them. Miranda thought that they were cute but the boys weren't so sure.

Then they saw a blue cape with red and green markings made with a primitive design on it like a map. The people looked a lot like Seth and Sen. They seemed afraid of the lights but they still had a portal keeper. They asked the light being where it had come from. As far as they knew only one dragon ever ventured to that dimension to exchange energy.

Sen and Seth wanted to meet the dragon. So the ball of light floated off to find her. As they looked from one treasure to the next, Miranda noticed that the boys' skin was starting to glow like hers. She asked them if they noticed anything different about her. As they looked at her, an expression of wonder and surprise came over their faces as they noticed her skin then they noticed theirs too.

Sen and Seth both had to use the bathroom also so Miranda showed them where it was.

Then she went to get their breakfast before they started in on the day's lessons. The balls were again very interested in the food that they had. Most of them had heard of food but had never seen it. They couldn't understand that there was no energy exchange that went on in the process. As she was preparing it they hovered so close that she was covered by multi color lights. They began extending their beams into her and connecting to her consciousness. It was truly wonderful to feel the unconditional love of the balls and in that instant to have all the knowledge of the universe and all the dimensions. As they withdrew so did the knowledge. The feeling of love still lingered as she kept preparing the food.

By the time Sen and Seth arrived back there all clean and glowy, she was done. For a few moments she was quietly still taking in all the things that had just happened to her. Then she just burst into talking. The words tumbling out so fast that Sen and Seth could hardly understand her, but they were getting the gist of it.

She explained how the balls of light exchanged energy with her and how, when they did it she knew everything in the universe. But when they left, she could only remember the experience.

Seth and Sen wanted to try it too. Kali had gone off to sniff and see if there was anything she would like to eat. The boys immediately asked the balls if they could do what Miranda had done with them. The balls had to go get new balls of light because they could only exchange energy once in a while. So off they floated and, in a few minutes a whole bunch of balls came flying in. Apparently, they were just as eager to try this as the boys were.

Vaishru also came to watch as they began the connections. This was rarely done between physical beings and light beings. It had never been done in their dimension. As it was happening, Ashtar came in to watch the joining.

As the connecting began, the boys started to glow and the balls became more solid.

It was amazing to watch the transformation, as the knowledge of the universe flowed into the boys. Their bodies filled with light, then slowly it was over and the balls started to withdraw. They felt heavy, but happy for the experience.

The boys seemed very floaty and quiet, just like Miranda was at first. Then they began to burst into talking as fast as they could. Ashtar tried to calm them as they all were chattering, and Kali started racing around the room from all the excitement. Ashtar finally floated above and let things run their course. After the excitement died down, it was time for another lesson.

Ashtar was to be the teacher for the day and the lesson was on transforming things. They all were instructed to get their feathers out. The feathers had changed, being back in their own realm, and had become brighter and more opal-like in color. Each feather had its own unique opalescent. Seth's feather was a pale turquoise blue with golden specks, Miranda's was a fiery orange with gold and sky-blue specks, and Sen's was a deep purple with pink's golds and blues in it. They all were marveling at how each feather could look so different from the each other when they all had come off the same bird.

Ashtar explained how each feather was taking on characteristics of its owner and in this realm that was amplified. He told the children to look at their skin and, to their amazement, they were starting to look like their feathers. They hadn't even noticed from being so excited about the joining of energy. Now they were instructed to merge their feathers.

As the light appeared, they were all told to concentrate on making a hat appear. It was to be brown with points on the front and back, and the brown was to be soft and fluffy. As they connected the picture in their minds an image emerged, and in the blue light of the feathers, a brown hat appeared. It was of the softest material any of them had ever seen or felt. They were amazed at how solid and soft it was. As the energy faded away, the hat stayed and Sen wanted to keep it. Seth wanted one too, so they made another one, then Mieanda wanted one too so a third one was made.

They were thrilled to be able to create things, so they started to enthusiastically practice making things. Ashtar watched, very pleased that they were able to pick this up so quickly and seemingly without any effort. The reason for this was there was no jealousy or envy among the three. That made life very wonderful and opened them to a whole new realm of being that wouldn't have been accessible had they had any hidden ill feelings.

After a great day of making things, all different kinds of things: statues, jewelry, even food which they ate along with what they had brought in their pack; they finally started to get tired. Ashtar told them they were done and that he was very pleased with their progress. Now was time to rest because tomorrow would be their last day there and it was going to be a very busy day for all of them. As they snuggled in their balls of light, filled with love and contentment, Kali ran around to each of them as they drifted off to sleep. They all were very happy with a calmness floating off each one of them.

Metuluso was off with Tibaru learning all the things about being a dragon of light.

She was connected with the balls of light, exchanging energy with them. Which, for her, was as great of a wonderment as it was to the children. After the experience, her skin and eyes whirled — in colors. Her eyes became hypnotic and dazzling all at once and her skin started shifting from shades of blue to green to golden to red to purple. It was an amazing sight to see. Tibaru was pleased to see that a dragon of the physical world could adapt to being in this realm. It was good news for both dragons to know. That meant more dragons could come and exchange knowledge and become what they truly were meant to be: keepers of all wisdom, of all times, and of all dimensions. This was a great thing.

The other light dragons were coming to see the transformation and the joy that was spreading filled the area, calling to all the light beings and dragons like a magnet.

There was high rejoicing as Metuluso disconnected from the balls. She, unlike the children, retained all the knowledge of the ages. She now knew what had happened to the people of Seth's village and where to find them. She also knew that they would have to wait for their job on this and all planes were far greater than finding the lost people.

Finding the lost people was just there to get them to begin the quest and learn of the dimensions. They were to be the first people to be dimension travelers; never before had this been done. They had been especially picked by powers much greater than all to fulfill this task. Each one of the travelers had a special purpose which was evolving with their training. Metuluso now saw clearly all that was and all that is and all that will be.

She had changed; she was now a being half of light and half of solid. Gone was her desire for flesh, she no longer needed that to exist. Her need to protect the children was stronger. She could now clearly see that they would need her in the weeks and years to come. It would be very important as they learned to navigate the dimensions. Metuluso never thought that she would be the one dragon. There had been whispers among the dragons of one dragon becoming a dragon of light to lead the way for the other others to transcend their plane of existence and go to another plane, but she had never dreamed it would be her. Metuluso had never dreamed that this would have happened to any of them.

Chapter 20

S wela was busy with her charge, taking very good care of her. The love between them was growing stronger, as was the bond between them, also. Nobody could separate them. Anything that Swela did, Orrusanu followed. When Orrusanu was hungry, the balls of light would appear and exchange energy with her and she was hungry a lot. Swela loved to be in the middle of the balls of light and feeling their love. She called them the love balls. They would sing to her and call to her and she would jump for joy as Orrusanu would change colors and hues.

Fern started coming over to visit and see how the baby was doing. Swela loved to have Fern come and visit. She was very happy to have attention from Seth's girlfriend, and not to be considered a pest. Fern met Swela in Swella's family's kitchen. They had a big wooden table with benches around it and a counter with all sorts of jars and bottles of things. Most of the jars were full of things that Joel made from what they grew in the garden.

Now that the balls of light were coming, her garden was going crazy. Things were growing bigger, the colors were brighter, and things tasted better. The plants were responding to the balls of light, also, it seemed. It was unexpected how things were changing just by having Orrusanu around. The people were no longer afraid of the balls of light. As people walked through the streets, the balls would appear and float around them. It seemed to be a very harmonious arraignment that was happening now that the people weren't afraid of the balls of light.

Fern was still a watcher, the winds still blew, and things were still being blown into their dimension. Things were calm now. It had been about a week since all the trouble had begun. It had rained some and the charred grasses were starting to grow back. Things were starting to feel normal again. Everyone was getting used to seeing Swela and the baby dragon wandering around the village, as she was showing the baby everything there was to see.

There was a steady stream of visitors dropping by Joel and Ty's house just to say "hi" and get a closer look at the dragon. She seemed to hypnotize everyone she came in contact with. They just couldn't get enough of her. Joel was busy trying to get things done from the harvest. There seemed to be even more things to do with all the guests just dropping in.

Swela just wanted to be with her dragon and wasn't that excited to be the center of attention anymore. She started to take Orrusanu out into the garden to play and they would play catch the light spheres and hide-and-seek in the garden, but they always found each other because the spheres would give them away by hovering over them. Neither one minded at all, since they just enjoyed being out in the garden in the fresh air and warm sun.

Swela, too, started to take on the glow of the lights as well as her brother and the others, though not as much as them because she was still in the physical plane and not in the realm of light. They were bonding so firmly that her mother was getting concerned. Swela was absorbing all the dragon knowledge that was in Orrusanu, and she was a very old dragon. Swela was like a little sponge and the knowledge just kept coming; she was a walking encyclopedia of dragon lore.

Her parents were happy for her, but also concerned. It seemed that most of their children were special light children and they were worried that other parents would get a little jealous about it. They needn't have had to worry about that. The other parents were happy that it was Joel and Ty's children and not theirs. Everyone seemed content.

Chapter 21

M eanwhile, back in the plane of light, the third day started. They all had learned how to match color to vibration and to open any portal they wanted. They also had learned how to create things from thought.

Today they were going to learn how to transform evil into love. That was to be the hardest of all challenges. To do that they had to feel complete love themselves towards whatever they were changing. That was easy when you had no thoughts of fear, but when you were afraid, it was harder.

Tashula was the teacher of the day. She was pure love. No negative thoughts flowed through her. As she drifted across to them, her warmth encompassed them. They had never felt anything like that before. The warmth and comfort made them melt, as all the love flowed through her, to them.

She explained the love for all things had to feel like that, even toward the evil that lurked in some of the dimensions. The love had to take over, and where there is light, darkness can't exist. This lesson was only going to show them how to create love, she couldn't show them more than that because she couldn't create evil.

So they started by learning how to create love.

In order to do that, they had to open their feelings up to let the light in. They started by shutting their eyes and looking for the light inside of themselves. That was a hard thing for them to do.

Miranda was the first to find a speck of light in her. Tashula told her to let it grow and grow until that was all she saw. The dot became a sun, then the sun became all. She was surrounded by the light as it became her. Her light blue skin let out a pure white light and she started to float. That shook her up and she lost all the concentration.

She plopped down very ungracefully.

Sen and Seth were just staring at her with their mouths hanging open. She said that it was kind of like putting the force fields around the plants when storms came in, but a whole lot more. She was at a loss for words to describe what had happened to her.

It was now the boys' turn to try it. Again, they closed their eyes to find the light. Sen was seeing colors floating by and Seth was just getting darkness. Then a thought from outside floated into their heads, to look at the center of the darkness. Out of that center, a tiny light of pure joy appeared, and from that joy came the unconditional love. From the love came the light. It just exploded on them as they lit up almost together as twin flames. In the middle was Kali, full of joy.

They began to float around the room as Kali wagged her crazy tail and did a silly dog dance, grinning from ear to ear.

Tashula told Miranda to bring in her light again, and as she did, the three of them floated above and merged into a triangle of pure love. Tashula just watched as the three experienced pure love for the first time. Kali was right in the middle, soaking up as much energy as her little dog self could absorb.

After about an hour, the children all floated down and Tashula explained to them what had happened and what they could do with it. She explained how, when evil was present, all they had to do was open up to pure love and not feel the evil and then it couldn't survive. That was easier said than done. If any fear was felt, it wouldn't work. They practiced all day long, going into pure love and joining their energies together.

The more they did it, the easier it got. The balls of light were interested and would help them if they were having trouble. It was a unique combination of things working together as they got the hang of it and it got easier as the day went on.

There was no night or day where they were, but a mellow evening seemed to be coming. They were getting hungry and thirsty. So Seth stopped and started to get the last of the food out as Metuluso came flying in with an enormous dragon half-eggshell.

She said that Tibaru had given it to her to give to Olif for some much needed light in his house. The blues of the eggshell twinkled in the light, little light beams were bouncing off everyone's hair. They were like little diamonds dancing in the light. It was a wondrous sight to watch as the evening progressed.

Tashula, Ashtar, and Vaishru came to visit as Seth brought out the food. The children ate and ate till they couldn't eat any more and drank long drinks from what had been given to them by the three elders, a water infused with the vibration of love.

Tashula explained what was going on with the children and how they had been brought together to be the first portal shifters among physical beings. As their bodies began to transition into multidimensional bodies, there would be times that they would feel extremely hungry. When doing energy work, it is difficult and can be tiring and you will be hungry when you are done. This would happen until their bodies had completely transcended to the next state of being.

She explained how the worlds worked and how they all fit into it. She also told them of the many places they would be visiting and some of the things they would encounter. But their first trip would be to go to another dimension with a vibration close to theirs.

The group was now ready to return to their dimension and time. For the dimension of light, time had no meaning. As the transformation of the five began, time was starting to have less meaning to them, also. When it was time to go, they really had no idea how much time had really passed since they had been in the dimension of light.

As the walked back to the portal the beings in the realm of light took on a whole new like to them. They could see every being with a new sight steeped in love which made the colors brighter and the sounds purer.

Tibaru walked with them back to the portal and Seth dialed in the dimension. It was with a joyful heart that they left the dimension of light. Kali was the first twinkle to hop through, then came Miranda, then Seth and Sen together, with Metuluso taking up the rear, holding the dragon half-eggshell. The balls of light followed them to the portal and sang a good-bye song, filled with love and hope, to the new portal travelers.

Olif was waiting for them at the portal and he was very glad to see them. He had missed their company. To the children, only three days had passed, but in Olif's and Seth's and Sen's time, three weeks had passed.

Metuluso had the dragon shell with her for Olif, who was very pleased with the gift and immediately started to plan where the shell was going to be placed.

Everyone was glowing with an opalescent other worldly light, their skin almost twinkling with rainbow hues of light. It was just enough to know something was different, but what?

Kali was even different—her fur had a rainbow glow. She was very happy to see Olif, since he was now a part of her family. She was her same over-joyous self as she bounded through this dimension.

Olif had a big meal prepared for the journeyers. He had picked two big cauliflowers and cooked them with onions and tomatoes and had cooked up a wild rice that had a slight taste of honey, with a wonderful cheese sauce to go over it all. Then there were nutty breads and goat cheese to eat with it.

Along with all that was a special dessert Miranda's mom had made and sent through the portal. She was always sending stuff now that she knew where her daughter was. It was one of Miranda's favorites; a pineapple-coconut pie with coconut cream topping.

It was one of the best meals they had ever had.

Life at that moment had never been better. It was good to be back from their adventure of being in the dimension of light, and now it was a time to relax for a few days, maybe even a few nights.

They were in good spirits, and as they ate, they chatted about all their experiences and talked of their adventures to each other and Olif.

Olif was impressed with what they had learned in a short period of time. They all took turns showing him the different things. He was really impressed at how you could go to the dimensions by the colors. That turned something random into something precise.

He wanted to make a chart of colors to dimensions. That could help him when he needed to help something or someone get back to their dimension. Metuluso said she would help him with that because she could remember. The children could only remember while the balls of light were connected with them.

They were anxious to see if they could connect with the light balls in their own dimension, so they called the balls of light to them like they had been taught, together as three, with Kali right in the middle. The balls of light started coming from all directions and soon the field was covered with them. It was almost as bright as the dimension of light.

The lights were all curious as to what was happening in the field. They all wanted to be part of this new thing. As the connections were being made, there was an exchange of energies and Olif was amazed as one of them began to glow and the lights started dancing around as the new energies from the solid forms flowed through them.

The children were surprised at how different it felt here. There was still the same unconditional love and all the knowledge of the universe came through, but just a little differently. In that moment, they knew what and where the lost people were.

The people seemed happy and content in their new home. Things there were quite different in that new home. Then, as soon as the connection was made, the images changed. When the connection was gone and the balls retreated back from the glowing children, they slowly faded as the images did. Their skin was a little more rainbow in color, their hearts a little more open to love.

But that was all that was left.

Olif was curious to see if he also could exchange energy with the lights. So he brought out his feather to call in some of the waiting lights. They danced with such enthusiasm that Olif didn't know what to think. Then they connected, first by the feather, then by a direct link. It was easy to make the connection because he was a gatekeeper.

For the balls, it was very different to connect with someone not from the light dimension. For them, it was a pleasant feeling, but they needed the light energy from that dimension to exist.

It was nice, and Olif also had all the knowledge of the universe in his brain for as long as the connection existed. Then it was gone and he was back to being just Olif.

Sen had the bright idea of having one person connect with the lights, then telling the others what they knew so that when they disconnected they could remember what they needed to know. Olif went to get things to write with while Sen and Miranda discussed who would hook up and who would listen. Seth said he would listen and Miranda thought maybe it would be best if she also listened.

Sen was to just sort out the information and start talking. Nobody had thought about talking while connected to the lights.

They were in the field where the portal was and, as the lights arrived, the portal began glowing as if it were getting ready to open. The colors started swirling and a pale blue green light started to take over. Nobody knew which dimension it was.

As it opened, Metuluso was right there with her glowing eyes, waiting and being very protective over the family she was becoming so close to. As the portal opened, everyone was standing there listening and watching, when out popped a little man with a long, red beard and pointy toed shoes with a very tidy suit.

He looked thoroughly confused and, when he saw the dragon standing there, he fainted straight away.

Everyone was just as shocked as him. Miranda ran to help him.

As he woke up, he had no idea where he was or what had just happened to him. Then he saw Metuluso staring at him, and he just passed out all over again.

Seth started to laugh, then Sen started to giggle, and soon Miranda was laughing. Olif managed to only smile but nearly. He was trying not to, so if the little man woke up again, he wouldn't be scared back to fainting.

He was very small, like Miranda but his skin was a ruddy pink color and with his red hair, he looked pretty red to everyone. His little suit was so cute; he looked very neat and clean.

Again he started to stir, and Metuluso backed off so as not to scare him into fainting again.

When he opened his eyes, all he saw was blue sky and four faces staring at him.

He started to quiver where he lay, but Olif stepped in and said something to him that only he understood. Then he started talking very quickly and agitatedly. Nobody could understand him.

His agitation scared the children and they remembered what they had been taught to do and brought in the pure love energy. He started to calm down to a point where they could hear his speech and start to understand him.

He said he was being chased by some very bad people who were trying to take away his gold. He had a bag he was hiding in his jacket that was full of gold. There were bars of gold and some coins.

Nobody in the group really cared about the gold he had, for they had learned so much about the universe that the gold wasn't very impressive to them. But the little man seemed worried about it.

Then he spotted Metuluso again and almost fainted all over again, but Olif kept him from fainting and assured him that the dragon would not eat him.

The balls of light had started to gather, but the little man didn't seem to notice them. They started to whisper to each other wanting to know who he was, where he came from. Seth told one of the balls of light the color of light in the portal was the dimension he had come from. The lights were all oohing and ahhing about it just like a pack of curious people.

Miranda and Sen started to laugh, and the little man (whose name was Merik), got very upset again. Olif told him he had to calm down and relax. Olif asked Merik where he came from and who was chasing him. Olif obviously had been through this many times before.

Merik told them he had come from a place where there were a lot of trees and he was from a small town built in the trees. His people loved the trees and were their caretakers. But sometimes big people like Sen and Seth would come and take things from them and did not trade.

He said that these people looked like Sen and Seth. The boys got their hopes up about that. They started to ask Merik where they came from and who they were. Merik said that these people had been around a really long time and were awful people that they had no real home and were always raiding peoples' villages and stealing what wasn't theirs.

By now, Merik was sitting in the field, talking as though he belonged there. He started straightening up his suit and plucking grass out of his beard. He really was a very careful, neat fellow.

As he chatted with everyone, the children were getting a feel for his dimension. He really didn't know about dimensions at all and it was quite the accident that had brought him there. He was very relieved to find out that the others couldn't follow him here.

As they talked, they got distracted from what they had been trying to do with the light.

Olif thought it would be good if they brought the little man back to his own dimension. It would be good practice for them. Olif and Metuluso remembered the color and Seth was going to be the one to open the portal.

It would be his first time to do anything like that, and Merik was afraid to go back. He thought that the bad people would be waiting there for him to come back. Olif told him that Metuluso would go through first, then Seth and Sen, followed by Miranda and him, with Kali in the rear.

That seemed to calm him down and Seth started to try to find the dimension through the revolving colors. It took a while to find the exact color. The first time nothing happened. It was just blank air—you couldn't even tell anything was there.

Olif tried to talk him through it. He knew how to open the portal and find some of the dimensions. So he started with telling Seth to clear his mind of all thought, then to see the portal there with the energy swirling around and project it out of his thoughts.

As he tried again, they could see energy starting to form, and then Kali barked and disappeared. Seth opened his eyes just in time to see Merik running away. Metuluso took about four steps and blocked him. She had a very threatening face on and a wisp of smoke came out of one nostril. That was all Merik needed to stop him in his tracks.

Olif was angry and the children looked astonished. They couldn't figure out why he was running away. He was shaking, even while Olif was scolding him and telling him that he couldn't stay in their dimension, that it wouldn't be good for him at all. He would die if he stayed there. It wasn't his time or place here.

That seemed to do it for him; he apparently didn't want to die, even more than he was scared of where he lived. He started to cry and Olif had to calm him down.

Everyone thought that he was a very strange little guy.

Seth started again to focus on the portal. It came quicker this time. The colors swirled, and Seth had to pick out the right color. He found that if he focused and concentrated on the right color as it appeared in the swirls, he could make the color grow.

Chapter 22

Metuluso knew how to find the way home and open the portal, so this was good practice for them. Seth got the color to grow until all of a sudden, the portal popped open and you could see the other world.

The colors were a little duller and the sun was a burnt orange that made things look different. They couldn't see anyone there—but Metuluso went through first just to make sure. Then everyone else went in. As Kali jumped through, the portal closed and they were gone.

Olif was alone again. He felt a little sad at being alone, since they had only been back a few hours before this had happened. He also was happy knowing that they were doing what they were born to do, even though it was happening so fast.

The children began to look around; they had to know where the portal was to get back home. Metuluso knew how to find it.

Metuluso told them she would fly up and take a look to see if there were other people or a caretaker, because other than them, the field was completely empty.

They waited and it was only a few minutes before Metuluso was back. She reported seeing some activities to the north, or the direction they thought was north. Merik said they were right. He thought that the Orlins must have left. They were the bad people that Merik was talking about.

Sen and Seth wanted to go explore. Kali was all over the place, checking out all the new smells. Merik said that he would take them to his home. They thought that it would be fun to see a tree village.

Merik led the way through the woods to a path. Seth thought it was strange that there was no portal keeper. Miranda reminded him that not all dimensions had portal keepers and that some dimensions didn't even know that there were portals. This seemed to be one of the dimensions that didn't know.

The trees looked familiar, almost like the trees in Sen and Seth's dimension, with just a few changes. As they walked through the forest, the trees seemed to get bigger and the tree trunks were smooth, with golden leaves waving on the branches. The trees got denser and the branches seemed to grow thicker and thicker. Paths appeared, and then houses, and all of a sudden they were in a clearing with all of the houses up in the trees.

Metuluso was flying overhead, keeping an eye on everything that was happening.

The children saw several bodies lying on the ground, and they figured that they must have seen Metuluso flying overhead and had fainted like Merik had done.

One brave soul walked out to greet them. Metuluso stayed out of sight for the moment. Kali was running up to the fainted people, licking them on the face to make sure they were alright. They were all short little people, with red hair like Merik.

Everything about the village was clean and orderly. The houses all blended into the trees and the walls looked like a blend of trunk and limbs at first glance. As they looked, closer they could see beautiful designs in the walls and branches. It was very rustic and very elegant at the same time. The leaves on the trees blended with the designs on the branches.

All the people were about three feet tall and had bright red hair. They all looked almost alike. The women were very well kept, with long red braids, and the men all had long red beards and cute hats.

The few who had fainted were starting to roll about and began to sit up. Kali was licking everyone around her because they were at her level. Merik was wondering what everyone was going to think of the dragon when she spiraled down to meet everyone. Merik could hardly wait.

Just as that thought went through his head, Metuluso came spiraling down, her skin glowing with the light that she had absorbed with their visit to the dimension of light.

She was in the process of changing over and transforming into a dragon of light. The children were also starting their transformation into beings of light, although none of them knew what was about to happen to them. The inner light in each had been fed through the balls of light connecting with them. This transformation allowed them to walk through the dimension more easily than another person. Miranda had a pale blue glow, while the boys had a golden glow, and Kali had a beautiful white light beaming through her. It was the unconditional love that dogs have for all living beings that brought that out.

Everyone looked with wonder at the dragon as she settled gracefully down on the ground in the middle of the circle. The greens and blues of her skin radiating out light of that color and the gold with flecks of rainbow color swirling in her eyes. Not one person fainted, which disappointed Merik just a bit. He had been hoping for some entertainment, but no such luck. Metuluso had sent out a vibration of safety to the people and they all felt totally safe.

Then, just at that time, a bunch of trees moved and out came a group of children who had been hiding, their eyes all big and round with expectation. Then everyone began to talk at once, but there was so much noise that nobody could understand a thing.

Then there was silence and Merik had to explain things to everyone about how he had been chased and then how he had fallen through the portal that he didn't even know was there. Then he had met all these people and he had wanted to bring them here to meet everyone.

The real reason was that he wanted a dragon with him to scare the bad people away. He, of course, didn't tell anyone that. He was hoping that this group of strangers would help free them of the terrors of the Orlins.

It was a lot for his people to absorb. They lived a simple orderly life and were easily frightened. Many of them were a lot like rabbits and were scared of most things. They had lived in terror of the bandits for many years.

Metuluso knew these weren't the lost people, even though the boys thought they might be. Kali was quite happy meeting all these little people, Seth and Sen felt like giants around them, and Miranda was simply quite content. She felt almost at home with all the people who were also her size.

There were about fifty people all together, ranging from babies up to elders. Everyone was neat and tidy, and very polite also.

Merik asked if anyone had seen the bandits, but nobody had. Metuluso told Miranda that she would go look for them. As she soared off, all the little red heads looked up in wonder at the half-translucent dragon.

Miranda was doing a good job explaining what was going on while the boys just hung back from the crowd. The people were getting hopeful that the bandits would be scared away, never to return.

Merik's people mostly kept to themselves, except for a few major holidays where they would all gather for festivals with other little towns. These festivals would last about a week before everybody would return to their villages and homes.

Now would be a really good time to chase off the bandits. Even though the Orlins had never found the homes of the little people, it would still be good to be rid of them.

After only a few minutes, Metuluso glided back. She had spotted the Orlins in the woods with three of the red headed people, who all looked pretty miserable.

There were about ten of the Orlins. They had pale brown skin and black, not brown, hair, and Metuluso was quite sure they hadn't seen her.

Metuluso told the children this would be a good time to practice banishing evil with unconditional love. They thought this would be a good thing also. How else could you get practice?

So they hopped on her back, with Sen holding Kali, and they took off to find the bandits.

As they approached, Metuluso swooped down just enough to scare them. It worked quite well and Metuluso thought it was great fun. Then she swung around and came to a landing with a little puff of smoke, again just enough to put a little fear into them. It got all their attention.

The leader was a very arrogant man, whose name was Rectas, and he wasn't a very nice individual.

No one moved as he swaggered over to the three of them. Kali gave him a low warning growl that none of them had ever heard before and that stopped Rectas in his tracks.

Then he spoke in a smooth silky voice, a voice not to be trusted. He politely asked what he and his friends could do for the travelers.

Seth responded, nothing special, they were just flying over on the dragon and thought it might be amusing to meet some of the local people in this area.

Seth was trying to be just as arrogant back to Rectas. He had seen his dad doing that to strangers at home and it seemed to work. It took Rectas by surprise. He wasn't used to other people not being afraid of him.

Miranda and Sen were starting to gather the energy of love from the orbs of light that had been following them.

The orbs in this dimension were rarely seen. As they moved about these visitors, the orbs were very aware of the fact that the five visitors knew of their presence and even invited a joining with them.

As the orbs started to join with the five of them, a golden glow started coming off of them, forming a huge orb that even the bandits couldn't miss. As the light spread, a darkness started swirling and the gold light of love swept over all, and nobody could move as the dark was banished.

Not even a shadow remained as the golden light took over. The orbs were wildly excited, as something like this had never happened here. They were busy singing and talking to everyone.

The bandits started breaking down and weeping as all the anger and rage was swept away from them, and the poor little redheaded captives didn't know what to do as they had all their fear washed away and the love took over.

After about twenty minutes or so, the light started to withdraw as quietly as it had come, singing a soothing song for all to hear.

Rectas was in a heap, sobbing hysterically. He had never felt so much love in his life, and forgiveness of all the evil he had done was too much for him. He was broken, along with the rest of his gang. There would be a lot of healing to be done within him and his cohorts.

Seth began talking, still glowing from the aftermath of it all. He explained in a kind, wonderful voice what was to be done next. The bandits were to take their little captives back to the village and ask for forgiveness from the residents. Also, they needed to return everything they stole and ask what they could do to help. Seth said they would go with them and make sure everything went well.

The bandits were too much in shock to say anything in reply. They just gathered up all their things and started to follow.

The little people had recovered and were looking at the five of them as if they were gods. They were so filled with love and gratitude that they couldn't contain themselves.

Seth was overflowing with love and oneness with this world and, as the rainbows of light swirled through his skin, he didn't even know anything else but love existed.

As things calmed, down Miranda was the first to get her wits about her. She started heading back to the village, encouraging all to follow, with the bandits and loot in tow. Nobody argued.

Segru was one of the little people. He was about thirty and very neat with his green suit on and now all brushed off and tidy. The others were still dazed, but Segru seemed to be more of a leader than the rest. He started telling the others what to do, and they seemed to need that.

Even the bandits followed, meek as kittens. They were starting to sob uncontrollably again while carrying everything.

Seth, Miranda, and Kali walked with everyone, while Sen and Metuluso flew back to the village to tell everyone what had happened and to expect visitors.

As they walked along the paths, Miranda was amazed at all the different plants and insects that were there. There were some flowers that were dark purple with light blue stripes and had a most wonderful smell. They were fantastic, with large petals and graceful leaves surrounding them. Segru was by now quite talkative and was telling her all the names of the plants. It was hard to hear him over all the sobbing from the bandits.

Seth and Miranda seemed to have gained more wisdom than their years from the experience and tried to calm all the chatter. Finally, Miranda had had enough and made everyone sit down right in the middle of the path. She then had one ball of light connect with each person and send calming energy into each person.

It was quick, only about a thirty second burst, but just enough to quiet them. They all gasped at once and Rectus became a new person so quickly it amazed all of them. He wanted to swear allegiance to Miranda and Seth. They told him he needed to look after all the little people and protect them from any harm. That was his and his men's new mission in life.

Sen flew into the village with Metuluso and all the people crowded around them. It was Sen's job to explain that the bandits were headed here and the wee folk were very worried about them coming. It was going to take some doing to convince them any differently.

They were all absolutely terrified of these bandits and now they were coming into the village. Sen assured them that Metuluso would burn anyone to a crisp that would try to harm them. That seemed to comfort them somewhat, as streams of steam came out her nostrils as Sen said that.

Metuluso was having great fun at this, as she is a dragon, and sometimes it's just fun to be a mighty dragon for the good of all.

The little villagers began scurrying around, hiding everything they could, so as not to put temptation in the way of the thieves. All the women and children were hidden until they knew they were safe, since nobody wanted to take any chances. Everyone wanted to believe there would be peace now and they wouldn't live in fear anymore, but it was hard to really believe.

A group of elders decided they would go and meet the party before they arrived to determine if it was safe or not to let them into the village. That seemed to be a very practical solution. So the biggest and burliest of the elders took off in the direction from which Miranda and Seth were coming.

By now, the sobbing bandits had calmed down a lot, and some were even trying to talk to the little captives who were no longer captives. Rectus wanted to be the most helpful and was actually starting to get a bit annoying. It seemed built into his nature to try to control and have all attention on him, even if he was trying to be nice. None of the bandits really knew how to be nice, but they were trying.

Seth thought it was funny but didn't say anything. This was all new territory for him. He had seen his dad taking the role of leader but never did himself. Miranda was being so calm and collected that he thought she had been born to do this. He was looking at her thinking how wonderful it was that she was part of the group, when Kali started growling, then snarling, as a big animal came lumbering out of the woods.

It looked like nothing Seth had ever seen before. It had big feet that went into thick legs and had a half dog, half human face with pointed ears and a snout, big teeth coming up around the snout, and big green eyes that looked like shining emeralds. A light was coming out of those emerald eyes.

Seth, Miranda, and Kali just stood frozen and Segru chimed in that this was a *rigorsta*, and they are used for helping to carry heavy loads and to protect people from any harm. He walked up to this big guy and started to pet his snout as a deep rumble left him. The *rigorsta's* fur, which was black, then started to shine a blue light as if electrified by the touch.

Segru explained that only a few of his people had the touch. None of the bandits had ever seen the touch either. They were amazed. They said they only used them for food and that started a big debate about how you shouldn't eat these creatures and how you should love and respect them. Even though they looked fierce they weren't, unless frightened, then would kill just like any creature.

Kali was sniffing the *rigorsta* with caution. Miranda was looking at it with all the love of the balls of light and Segru was ordering all the little people up on the creature's back. They were going to go for a lovely ride.

The bandits were in awe, as they had never seen anything like that, even though they had been here a long time. As they started out again, the little ones were quietly gathering together and as they started on their ride, the talking started up again.

The bandits were scared of this thing and wouldn't go near it. Miranda wanted to ride on it just to experience it. Kali was by this time relaxed around the *rigorsta* and back to her old happy self, off running and exploring.

Metuluso and Sen also needed to let the people know the captives were safe and warn them they were having company so nobody would faint. Metuluso had flown over the traveling group to make sure everything was going well and no bandit had reverted back to being bad. Everything seemed to be going well, she was satisfied with what she saw and headed back to the tree village with her report. Which made the villagers feel better and braver.

The bandits were still apologizing as they walked next to the *rigorsta*, that they had been so small minded that they had never realized they could live and learn from their neighbors. It was great how such a transformation could come just from the love that the balls of light could give.

It was a wonderful lesson to Miranda, Sen, Seth, and Metuluso. If this sort of adventure was their destiny, all the lessons would come in handy.

They were learning not to be scared in the face of evil, along with knowledge of what the balls of light were capable of doing. This was wonderful for them. They were learning a lot of good things on this little trip and helping a world come to peace.

The little redheaded people still weren't sure of the bandits, but they were starting to feel a little more comfortable, since they were all up on the back of the *rigorsta* who would protect them.

Miranda happily chatted with Segru about his special talent of calling the *rigorsta*. As they went through the forest, Seth was looking at all the strange plants and smelling all the smells. It seemed that his senses had become sharper as his body was undergoing its transformation.

It seemed very much to Miranda that Segru's talent was very much like her own with the dragons. The only difference was that dragons bonded with one person and the *rigorsta* didn't. *Rigorsta's* were more of a free spirit and helped only if they chose to. Segru could talk to them through mind pictures, as they didn't have a language like the dragons. They projected thought pictures, which was hard for a speaking person to get used to.

As they were meandering back to the village having a pleasant chat, Seth was starting to see that things in this dimension weren't that much different than in his. It was sinking in that this was going to be his new life. He was wondering if he would ever be able to go back to his old life, and wondering about Fern, if she'd be left behind, too.

The meeting with the two groups went well. The bandits were very sorry and the little people were very forgiving, especially for all that they had been put through at the hands of the bandits. But the bandits were not yet allowed to enter the village. It was decided that the former bandits had to prove themselves before being welcomed into the village. That was acceptable to all.

As the travelers left the village and went back to the portal, Merik went with them and marked where the portal was and, with the promise that they would return if the bandits misbehaved, he said a sad good-bye to them all.

The bandits had been told that if they fell back to their old ways that Metuluso would be there in a flash to turn them into crispy critters. They all said that they were changed forever. None of them could believe that they had behaved like that in the past. With that, they were off and through the portal and home once again.

Chapter 23

O lif was happy for them to be back and told them that they could have a few days off to rest and recuperate before the next training.

The boy's wanted to go home after a few days at Olif's house and Miranda wanted to go with them. They were only to be gone for a day and be back that night.

Metuluso flew them to the village and both Seth's and Sen's moms were happy to see their boys, along with Miranda.

The three of them were met by many happy people who wanted to know what they had been up to. The color of their skin was a give-away that something was very different. Fern was the most interested in what was happening to them because she didn't want to be left out of the adventure any more than Sen had wanted to be left out.

Seth told Fern to let the lights link with her. He showed her how that was done. As she tried it and felt the love, her whole person changed. Seth told her also to hang out with Swela and the baby dragon, who wasn't so tiny any more as the lights kept her full of energy and she was quite a happy baby dragon.

Orrusanu wanted to know about her family in the dimension of light and insisted that she get a full report about her dimension. Her knowledge was growing by leaps and bounds and it was all being passed on to Seth's sister who was now wise beyond her years and was transforming into another being of light.

Swela would be the first dragon rider on a dragon of light. Soon she would be able to ride Orrusanu, and that was a day she could hardly wait for. Swela remembered Metuluso's promise of giving her a ride and insisted that she get to go on one.

Seth took her up on Metuluso's back and they went for a short ride. Swela seemed to be completely at home on the dragons back like she had been doing it her whole short life. She was in complete control of the whole thing, or so she thought. Metuluso just thought it was humorous that this little girl was ordering her around, somewhat like Miranda had at her age. Orrusanu flew along with them since she was getting her flight skills back and her body was getting stronger day by day.

Orrusanu had now grown to the point that she could hardly fit into the house with Swela and Seth's parents were trying to figure out a new place where she could sleep. They knew something had to be done soon so an attachment to there house was being made to accommodate the new member of the family.

Fern and Miranda went off together and had some girl time, as Miranda was missing being with some female company. They had a good time and Fern learned more from Miranda about being a portal jumper. Someday, she wanted to travel from dimension to dimension, too.

Right now, her job was to keep the village safe. She knew her job was important, but she missed her friends, too. The day went too fast for the three of them and, as night approached, they headed to Metuluso and got ready to take off.

Sen's and Seth's parents were sad that their boys were leaving again after such a short visit, but there were promises that the next visit would be longer. Then they were off with another big basket of goodies from both of the moms.

Olif was happy to have them back and they were happy to be in their own beds again. They had installed the new eggshell dome from the land of light and it glowed along with the other eggshell in the pale light of evening. It was a welcome sight to the three weary travelers.

The next day the group wanted to link with the orbs again to find the lost people. They started out with Sen linking and Olif, Seth and Miranda listening and taking notes on what Sen had to say. The questions had been carefully thought out so nothing would be forgotten.

As Sen linked and the knowledge of the universe came flooding into him. When the questions began at first it was hard for Sen to sort things out but he quickly got the hang of it and was able to tell them where the lost people were located and how they were. To everyone's surprise they were very happy and content and not interested in returning home. The original people who were blown away were all long gone and their childrens, children only knew that place as their home. So the need to find them wasn't as urgent as they had thought.

That made it much easier for now they would be free to learn the lessons that their true destinies were meant for.

After another couple of days, the next adventure was going to start. The children would go to the portal, along with Metuluso. They would begin another lesson of finding colors to other dimensions knowing that the start of the real journey has begun.

The End

Made in the USA
Coppell, TX
23 November 2020